MUM'S WOODS

BASE FEAR: BOOK 3

S.C. FISHER

Copyright © 2023 by S.C. Fisher

Published by Raven Tale Publishing

All rights reserved.

This book may not be duplicated in any way without the express written consent of the publisher, except in the form of brief excerpts or quotations for the purposes of review.

The information contained herein is for the personal use of the reader and may not be incorporated in any commercial programs or other books, databases, or any kind of software without written consent of the publisher or author. Making copies of this book or any portion of it, for any purpose is a violation of United States copyright laws.

This is a work of fiction. Names, characters, places, and incidents either are the product of the author's imagination or are used fictitiously. Any resemblance to actual persons, living or dead, events, or locales is entirely coincidental.

ISBN: 9798389287587

❦ Created with Vellum

For Carol and Helen – the women who showed us how to discover new worlds through the turn of a page.

PROLOGUE

There is a tale that some folk tell
Of how young Agnes Tippett fell,
Of loose tongues and of prophecy,
Of murder and the twisted tree.

Beneath the soil she lies in wait,
For a chance to change her fate.
O'er her bones the worms do creep,
For evil rests, and she does sleep.

Yet if the witch should ever wake
The souls of seven she will take,
To pay the sum of Scratch's fee,
That he might set her spirit free.

So be you warned - be you wary,
Watch out for the red yew berry.
Should Aggie set her sights on you?
There is naught that God himself can do.

1

DAY 1 – 10:17 HRS

For almost three years I occupied the same seat in Mr. Friedman's History class. Not a lot changed in that time, from the broken blinds that allowed too much light in the afternoons, to the gum moulded to the underside of my desk, which I'd learned to avoid with my knees through experience.

Assigned seating could blow but I had it better than most since my two best friends sat within prime note passing distance - Tiff directly behind me and Charlie on my left. We were still caught more often than not. Even though Mr. Friedman could be a hard-ass, he had a soft spot for us girls: the ones who didn't tease him about his lazy eye, and always turned in our assignments on time. Although we racked up more than a few detentions for our shenanigans, Friedman never made a move to reassign our seats. When we were together, we were happy, and Mr. Friedman liked his favourite students to be happy, in that weird *'peace and love'*, soy-macchiato drinking, *'save the rhinos'* way that middle-aged teachers have about them. He was a pretty nice guy, who was mostly just grateful that we were passing old-school notes rather than filming *TikToks* in the middle of class.

We had some good times in History. Until we didn't. Until Charlie vanished without a trace.

Every October, about a week away from the fall holiday, Mr. Friedman would wheel a trolley into the room, and a collective moan that resembled the cries of the ravenous undead would ring through the class. The trolley housed a TV that was so square and awkward that it blotted out the teacher's desk plus half the whiteboard. We all knew what was coming next. *The video.* An actual, honest-to-God, VHS tape that Friedman fed into the mouth of his VCR beast – his eyes, including the lazy one, sparkling. To Friedman, that singular moment was better than a thousand Christmas mornings.

After years of the same History class with the same teacher, I could practically recite that tape word for word: the half-imagined, half-historically-accurate, tale of Agnes Tippett. Spoiler alert – there was no happy ending.

Maybe that's why I wasn't in the mood for it that morning, with my world spinning crooked on its axis, as it was. Our story – the mystery growing and spreading like poison ivy around our feet – had only been partially written, and I was so very afraid of how it might end.

Leaning back in my seat, fists clenched in my lap, I watched Mr. Friedman set up his show. He rubbed his hands together once the tape slid home into the slot, true glee replacing his typical stoicism. His excitement should have been infectious but only half my mind was present in the classroom with my body. The other half was off with my best friend. The one who hadn't come home.

Forty-eight hours. The crucial window they talk about, as if they know anything at all. Reality is, some people go missing - a handful of them return but most will never be found. The thought of Charlie being among the latter made me want to vomit over my desk.

"I understand that we might not be in the frame of mind for classwork today so I thought I'd honour our little tradition a bit early this year."

I glanced at the board, squinting at the date bunched in the top corner. October 10th. He was early, after all. Friedman droned on, his proper English accent clipping vowels and consonants left and right.

"It's almost Halloween and, as you all know by now, Mildenhall has a rather macabre history. Matthew Hopkins, the self-proclaimed..."

"Witchfinder General," the class recited, eyes rolling and shoulders heaving with sighs en masse. We'd heard it too many times before for any of it to spark interest.

Mr. Friedman managed a smile, regardless, and his gaze bounced over the rows of seats, desks, and bent heads. I heard the tell-tale ping of incoming messages, and he must have too, yet Friedman chose to let it go. His attention returned to the waiting TV. The remote - if such a creature had ever existed - had been lost at the dawn of time, so Mr. Friedman focussed on the line of buttons beneath the screen. Sunlight hit the glass and the dust motes flitting through the air were reflected on the domed surface. As the TV hummed, I felt a tap on my shoulder. I ignored it for a beat, watching as the familiar face of the actress cast as Agnes Tippett - way before I'd been born - blinked into existence.

I bided my time until Friedman had perched on an empty desk a row ahead, his arms crossed and his hands tucked into his pits. His back bowed after a moment, shoulders hunching, his relaxing posture indicating that he was losing himself in the drama. I didn't turn. Instead, I pushed my right arm backwards, palm upturned to the ceiling. The familiar weight of a piece of folded paper steadied my sprinting heartbeat. Prize retrieved, I unfurled the note in my lap, my eyes occasionally floating to Friedman, who was so fully absorbed in the title sequence of the documentary that an atomic explosion couldn't have disturbed him.

A downward glance brought Tiff's cursive into focus.

'Any news?'

My reply was blunt. I passed it back, one armed again. I had a tendency to write all in capitals and my words dwarfed Tiff's scrawl.

'STILL MISSING.'

Behind me, there was a sigh that might have been masking a sniffle, but I didn't dare try to comfort Tiff. Whilst Mr. Friedman was willing to overlook the occasional misdemeanour, he wouldn't stand for such a blatant disregard of his sacred annual ritual. Now, he was far too focussed on the screen, upon which I caught odd glimpses of my own reflection. It would only take a brief scene change and we would be caught red-handed. Detention was the last place I wanted to be with Charlie gone.

Another tap. I huddled over the desk, pretending to adjust my position, before reaching back and plucking the next note from Tiff's hand. She'd folded this one into an ostentatious rose. I picked it apart, petal by petal, with a shake of my head, revealing her message.

'Think she's okay?'

Friedman cleared his throat, loudly, and that was all it took to drag my eyes back to the TV. I couldn't tell if he was watching me or not, but he sat straighter and I lost the final shreds of my nerve. I balled the paper to shove it into my pocket.

I heard Tiff grumble in irritation, although it was more difficult to pick out her little huffs and puffs over the screaming that had struck up at the front of the class. I shuddered, the chill of the room sweeping my spine like a breath on bare skin, despite my sweater. I was in no mood to witness Agnes' cruel fate today, nevertheless, I couldn't seem to look away whilst it played out.

"1645. A time of great hardship for the poorest of England's inhabitants. Agnes Tippett, the nineteen year old daughter of an aging widow, is among them."

Someone yawned so obnoxiously that their jaw cracked. Mr. Friedman shot a nasty look over his shoulder at the perpetrator when a burst of laughter echoed around the class. I didn't look away from the screen.

The actress playing Agnes Tippett sported a voluminous perm that seemed to make it tough to perch her white bonnet on her head. Still, the costumer had tried, and the cap bobbed on the crest of fake Agnes' puffed hair like a galleon riding the waves. It should have been funny. It was every other year. Usually, Charlie was one of the first to laugh at the parade of mullets, pastel eyeshadow, and shoulder pads on display in seventeenth century England. This time, it was different. It felt abnormal to find humour in anything.

The speakers buzzed, frazzled with dust and through age, muffling the voice that recounted Agnes' life.

"Official records show that Agnes earned a pittance tending land at several nearby farms. The work was arduous and sporadic, and Agnes was forced to compete with local youth for employment. Eventually, she would turn to a skill she had practiced since childhood as a means to supplement her income; a skill that would result in her cruel murder."

I wasn't a sensitive person but the word teased a shudder from me that rippled through my body in aftershocks. Considering the circumstances of Charlie's disappearance, murder was a concept I couldn't stand to dwell on. I wished with everything in me that Mr. Friedman would turn the damn video off and release class early. I glared at his back, eyes narrowed, doing my best to convey my discomfort with will alone. Friedman shuffled on his perch and, hopeful, I mirrored the shift from mine.

Unfortunately, he settled back quickly, legs crossed and head tipped at a better viewing angle.

Onscreen, fake Agnes and her perm poured over a bowl filled to the lip with water. The actress squinted at the prop whilst trying her best to look both mysterious and captivating. The crinkle in her brow and the set of her jaw made her look constipated, instead. A few more giggles and snorts prompted Friedman to whip around with a well-honed expression of warning. The class quieted, though I wished they wouldn't. I'd have preferred to drown out the video with its rambling monologues.

"The women of Mildenhall gathered often and in secret at the Tippett home, where they would beg Agnes to peer into their futures. In exchange for a coin, a bag of flour, or a few apples, she would often oblige."

"Agnes was a grade-A moron."

The voice, rather than the observation, startled me, and the legs of my chair squealed against the floorboards when I jumped. Friedman jabbed the pause button, freezing the image of Agnes and her bowl. On the surface of the water, the SFX people had superimposed the picture of a woman. A shawl circled her shoulders and she held a cloth to her lips, the dark makeup ringing her eyes and sweat speckling her brow serving as a bad omen. I knew this part of the legend as well as any other: Agnes had predicted the death of one of the townswomen and sealed her own fate in the process. So they claimed.

"Would you like to explain your take on the story, Isaac?"

Mr. Friedman tented his fingers in front of his nose as he stared down the aisle at the kid who'd interrupted. Isaac Kohli smirked, more than happy to oblige with the spotlight beam focussed on him. One hand raking through his thick, black hair, he shot a glance to his right at Phoebe Greenwood, who flushed from ears to toes. Isaac had been hung up on Charlie a term before, but things change when you're missing and already presumed dead by half the school.

"Sure, sure. The way I see it, Agnes was beyond stupid. I mean, the whole country was going crazy, worrying about demons and witches and stuff. Why would you set up shop as a fortune teller and expect people not to freak out about it?"

It was a valid point, at least, and Mr. Friedman appeared to consider it for half a second before he clapped back.

"The prospect of starvation can be a powerful motivator. Perhaps it seemed to Agnes to be her best chance of survival. Any able-bodied person in the village could have found work at the farms, but this was something that only Agnes could do. It made her special."

"It got her killed," countered a girl from the back row. Whispers of agreement followed and Mr. Friedman was forced to concede.

"Yes, it did."

"Guess she should have seen that coming, then."

Isaac's bark of laughter was joined immediately by most of the other students in the room, who were so far disconnected from Agnes Tippett that they could extract humour from her death. I chanced a peek over my shoulder at Tiff, finding her staring mute at her desk as if she was trying to drill holes through the wood with her pupils. I knew, like me, that she was thinking of Charlie.

Friedman flapped his hands at the room, urging everyone to pipe down. They were slow to follow orders, full blown laughter receding to chuckles only when his brows knitted.

"Most local historians believe that Agnes was clever when it came to the nature of her prophecies," Mr. Friedman interjected, a sour grimace his sole display of disapproval. "If we consider modern day equivalents to soothsayers, then we see certain patterns emerge in their predictions. For example, they may tell you that you're due to travel, or that you'll meet someone whose name begins with a particular letter, or that you'll consider a change of employment. Nine times out of ten, these ambiguous predictions stand a very good chance of being true. In the seventeenth century, there were certain other likelihoods: you have an admirer, your garden will flourish, you'll sell your lambs at market."

The last smatters of laughter died out. Whilst the video was definitely nothing new, Friedman's willingness to talk about it was, and he'd managed to unwittingly snare us with it. He appeared to realise as much, and his frown trickled away into a gentle smile that disturbed the glasses perched on the bridge of his nose.

"It's entirely possible that Agnes claimed to foresee a death set far in the future, but a combination of low mortality rates and bad luck saw a tragedy realised long before Agnes had considered it likely to be."

Perfect silence prevailed over the class. Not even Isaac continued posturing. I wondered if perhaps every one of us was turning over Agnes' choices and resultant misfortune, questioning what we might have done in her place. Mr. Friedman peered at his students in turn, probably astounded by our interest in the topic he'd fought to engage us with for years. Finally, the same girl spoke from the back, lips twisted into a half smile that was teasing but not disrespectful.

"So you don't believe Agnes could see the future for real, Mr. F.?"

It was his turn to laugh - a sound we'd barely heard in all the years he'd taught us. I guess it wasn't so easy to find things funny when you became the butt of most of the jokes.

"No, I don't, Alice."

"What about the rest of the legend?" Isaac pressed, his

expression more sombre than before. "Do you think Agnes is waiting in those woods, hoping for her seven souls?"

The question dumped a bucket of ice water down my shirt and I shivered so hard that all my limbs curled into my body. Like a spider, once it succumbs to death.

Mr. Friedman shook his head, something in his eyes cautionary. I thought he might have looked to me, bowed almost in the foetal position over my desk, but I could have imagined it.

"I don't think this conversation is entirely appropriate, Isaac. If you have questions then find me at lunch..."

A rap on the doorframe drowned out the rest. The door swung open soon after, without invitation. I swallowed the lump of awful discomfort that had risen in my throat, and Tiff's foot shot out to kick the back leg of my chair as if she'd lost control of her limbs. The principal – fleshy, white-haired Mrs. Doherty – stood in the doorway, flanked by two women who had the words *Ministry of Defence Police*' emblazoned on the shoulders of their luminous jackets. I reached under my desk for my schoolbag before anyone spoke – before the rest of them flinched. This was something I'd been expecting all morning. I didn't need to wait for the order.

Mrs. Doherty was the one to deliver it. "Tiffany Evans and Olivia Sibley? Could you girls come with me, please?"

Tiff's foot struck my chair once more. I swept my books into my open bag, deliberately avoiding eye contact with everyone and anyone that looked my way. I could feel the pressure of many stares – scores of pinpricks piercing my skin.

It was our turn.

2

DAY 1 – 10:55 HRS

"Are we in trouble? Should our parents be here? Or, like, a lawyer?"

Tiff squirmed in her seat - a maggot on a hook - a glint of undisguised terror flashing in her hazel eyes behind the lenses of her glasses. It was the first time in our lives that either one of us had spoken to the cops. Though we both knew we'd done nothing wrong, there was something intimidating about staring at those uniforms.

The first officer offered a smile, not amused or reassuring, but not really hostile either. She seemed more bored than anything. Her colleague drummed her pen against her notepad whilst we waited for Mrs. Doherty to return with the tray of coffee she'd promised.

All morning the police had been working their way through a list of students and teachers who had regular contact with Charlie. I knew, as one of her closest friends, that I'd be on there. It had still felt like a dip in an ice cold lake to be called on.

We'd been led to a vacant art class on the second floor. The room was being used as a base of operations for the cops since most of the art teachers favoured the studio that had recently been added on to the school.

"Nobody is in trouble. We're trying to find out if anybody might have an idea where Charlotte would go. Her parents are very concerned for her wellbeing," said the second officer as she clicked the top of her pen and began to scribble in her notebook.

"Charlie," I corrected, reflexively.

The woman – she'd introduced herself as Constable Ford – pursed her lips as she studied me.

"You two are close?"

I nodded, rubbing my palms against my thighs in an effort to scrub the sweat from my skin. Reminding myself that I had nothing to be worried about was proving difficult.

"We all are," said Tiff, her hand sidling across the divide to rest in the small of my back. I breathed a sigh, relieved by the contact.

"We've known each other since I came to England three and a half years ago."

Whilst Constable Ford added to her notes, Mrs. Doherty stumbled through the door with a tray.

"I managed to ferret out some biscuits from the staff room," she declared, clearly impressed by her own ingenuity.

She set the tray down a little hard and it skittered across the table, spilling coffee over the rim of the mugs. Most of them were plain white, except for the one Mrs. Doherty reached for, which was emblazoned with the words *'Teaching Is My Superpower'*. I cringed internally from second-hand embarrassment and shoved a cookie in my mouth to better resist a sly comment.

"Where were you before England?" asked the other officer - Constable Lyndhurst - whilst she dunked her cookie in her coffee. I'd never understand why they called them 'biscuits' in

England. The word made me think of bacon, thick gravy, and breakfast at my grandma's house.

"My dad was based at Peterson in Colorado."

She beamed then slurped hard from her cup before she responded.

"My cousin lives in Florida."

Expectantly, she waited for me to comment on the perceived connection. I barely restrained myself from pointing out that Colorado is over a day's drive from Florida.

"That's cool," I offered, after a long and uncomfortable pause. Then, I reached for my coffee and tipped the mug to my lips so I didn't have to make small talk anymore.

As Mrs. Doherty hauled up a chair, Ford and Lyndhurst pulled out their impossibly long list of questions, and fired them off at us like they'd watched too many police procedurals. Tiff and I took turns answering. I could sense her vibrating next to me, a mix of unease and sadness causing her body to thrum with an extra pulse. She paused to remove and clean her glasses on her sweater three times – a sure sign she was as jittery as I was.

"Did Charlie suggest that she was having problems at home before she left?"

"No. Her parents are super nice. She's really close to her sister."

A box checked, a theory shelved.

"Did Charlie talk to you about running away? Even if it was a long time ago, it might help with the investigation."

"Never." My turn to field. "She talked about leaving for college. That was it."

More scribbling, a few dissatisfied hums. Mrs. Doherty listened attentively, her thumb curled into her mouth so that she could gnaw on the skin next to her nail.

"Was Charlie feeling well the last time you spoke to her? Well in herself, I mean."

I translated as *'was Charlie likely to hurl herself off the nearest bridge'*. I elected to let Tiff answer before I snapped. Charlie would never consider hurting herself. She loved life too much. Besides, she would have reached out to me if things had gotten bad like that. At least, that's what I told myself. I hadn't exactly been as present as I once was, with school, work, my music, and family life eating at my time. Back when I'd first met Charlie, we used to talk every night on our phones or online. During the first weeks of our senior year, that had trickled away to once - maybe twice - a week.

"She seemed fine the last time I saw her," said Tiff, sounding far too unsure for anyone's liking.

Lyndhurst looked up from her partner's notes, catching Tiff's eye.

"When do you think you may have last had contact with Charlo... Charlie?"

Tiffany squinted, finger twirling through a strand of her hair as she considered the question. The overhead light caught a streak of purple interwoven through the brown. Tiff changed her hair colour the way most people change their socks.

"Maybe Thursday? I didn't come to school Friday so…"

She trailed off, shooting me a glance that both officers intercepted. They were evidently curious.

"I was supposed to meet her on Saturday. She was going to come by the ice cream parlour before I finished work. We were maybe going to the movies."

Except we didn't because Charlie had never shown. Not while I was wiping down counters, or putting away leftover stock, or mopping the floor. I'd waited twenty minutes past the end of my shift, perched on the edge of the concrete fountain that scars the centre of the BX Exchange. I guess it's supposed to make it feel more like a real shopping mall.

It wasn't like Charlie to blow anyone off, especially me, so I'd naturally started to worry. I called then messaged when I was sent straight through to voicemail, but I didn't reach Charlie that night.

"When she didn't show, I... I went home. I thought either she was mad at me about something or she had some kind of family emergency. I was tired so..."

My voice petered out into nothing on the back of my sentence so that the final words were a hoarse whisper. Shame. It hit me like a ten tonne truck, not for the first time since I'd learned that I could have raised the alarm about Charlie's disappearance on Saturday night. If only I'd gone looking, knocked on her door, asked to see her. The Hills hadn't noticed until Sunday when they'd realised Charlie's bed hadn't been slept in, and that nobody seemed to know where she was at.

Ford leaned across the table, a flash of sympathy crossing her face as she touched the back of my hand.

"It's okay. I'm sure we all would have done the same," she consoled me whilst Tiff leaned closer into my side.

I sucked in a breath to cover my sniffle and nodded. There was no changing it; it was done. When Charlie had needed me the most, I'd failed her. All I could do going forward was try not to make the same mistake.

"Can't you track her phone or something? She's got one of those watch things, too." The suggestion came from Tiff, who was working her way through each of her nails, nibbling them down to the quick.

"We tried. She didn't have her watch with her, and the phone stopped working just after seven pm on Saturday evening."

Charlie should have been making her way to the parlour

about then. None of us had the faintest idea where she'd decided to go instead.

"There's one thing." I raised my eyes from the scratches littering the desk to Lyndhurt's face. "It might help."

"Anything you can think of," Ford chipped in, and Lyndhurst managed a smile that almost came off as encouraging. They were doing better, I had to admit.

"Charlie told me she met someone over the summer. Online. Some guy that hung around these paranormal investigation forums she liked. She was pretty into him. I think... she said he told her that he was falling for her. She talked about them maybe meeting up. I told her not to but Charlie can be... stubborn."

He knows all about urban legends and junk. He only lives a half hour away, can you believe it? I could hear her voice, clear as a bell, chiming in my head. *He said he loves me. I think he's the one.*

I should have tried harder to put a stop to it, nipped it in the bud before it had the chance to take root. I could have threatened to tell her parents or Coach Rhodes.

I didn't.

Mrs. Doherty made a noise of disgruntled disbelief in her throat, and Tiff shot her a look that contained the power to kill. I ignored them both, too focussed on the cop in front of me who was hanging off my words.

"Do you know if this potential boyfriend has a name?"

Ford's eyebrows inched to her hairline as they arched. I couldn't hold her disbelief against her. The whole school had sat through the lectures and warnings a million times. We knew the cautionary tales as well as we knew *Cinderella* or *Hansel and Gretel*. Never agree to meet with some random you meet online, unless you want your face plastered all over the ten o'clock news whilst the cops comb the local farmland with sniffer dogs.

"She never told me his real name. His screen name was *Lost-Boy666*. That's all I know."

I left the makeshift interview room with the self-inflicted mantle of 'traitor' heavy round my neck. Tiff walked by my side, her arm threaded through mine, but she remained silent as we headed outside. I wondered if she was judging me, or else considering if I'd spill her secrets as quickly at the first sign of trouble.

We found Hayley and Rose waiting for us at our usual bench, both bundled in thick coats and scarves, yet shivering against the October wind. Hayley was the first to hop off the bench as we opened the door leading into the quad, which nestled in the middle of the language classrooms. The space was originally intended as a memorial garden for faculty and students, but lack of use had seen the addition of picnic benches. Aside from a scattering of dwarf trees accompanied by brass name plaques, the garden was otherwise empty. We were among only a handful of students to make use of it, purely because me and Charlie had enjoyed the peace.

"How are you doing?"

Tiff lunged to tug Hayley into her arms. They embraced, Hayley burying her face in Tiff's shoulder as she sucked in a couple of steadying breaths.

"Not great," whispered Hayley, drawing away but maintaining her grip on both of Tiff's arms. "It's awful at home. Mom cries all day and Dad hasn't slept."

My features scrunched, sympathy and sorrow crumpling my face into something unrecognisable. Hayley was Charlie's baby sister, younger by two years almost exactly to the day. Their birthdays fell less than a week apart so they usually held some kind of joint celebration. Last year, it was ice skating followed by a sleepover with an outdoor projector. We'd watched *Alien* on the side of the Hill home that faced the backyard and eaten s'mores that Mrs. Hill had nuked in their microwave.

"Have you been interviewed yet?"

Rose drew up at Hayley's side, wrapping a possessive arm around her waist as she stared at me and Tiff in turn. The breeze tossed a strand of feathery, blonde hair into her face and she blew a furious breath to dislodge it. When her eyes were no longer obscured, I could see the spark of dislike she reserved for us.

Rose Anderson was one of my least favourite people I'd met since moving to England, and I got the impression the feeling was more than mutual. She was the only native amongst our group of six, and also the only one whose family didn't live in the on-camp married quarters. Both her dads worked for the Royal Air Force - not the USAF - so their house was situated about a quarter mile from the fence, in a street reserved solely for military personnel. Sometimes, I wondered if this was the source of her dislike for those of us who weren't Hayley. Did she feel disconnected from the group? Did she worry we thought we were somehow better than her? Or was she really just sore that we diverted Hayley's attention away from her?

Rose was Hayley's friend, first and foremost, and the rest of us tolerated her because of it. Hayley was a lot of fun, not to mention Charlie's kid sister, and none of us could have imagined our group without her. Most of us probably would have happily imagined it without Rose, though.

"We just came from the cops." Tiff's voice was tight and I wondered if she'd noticed the look of distaste Rose levelled at us, too. "Hopefully, between all of us, they can piece together where Charlie's gone."

There was a lot of nodding, then some shuffling as each of us searched our failing brains for something appropriate to say. In the end, it was Rose that spoke, but only to Hayley.

"I have to go. Daddy is picking me up for my dentist appointment in ten minutes. Call me tonight, okay?"

I ignored Tiff miming gagging motions behind Rose's back as she wrestled Hayley into a hug. I might not have been president of the Rose Anderson fan club but I definitely didn't need to be adding to Hayley's stress levels by picking fights with her best friend. With Rose sashaying out of the quad, and Tiff darting off to her next period, Hayley and I were left alone amongst the half-empty rows of soil and cracked alabaster pots. We stared at each other, then Hayley melted against my chest with a sob that clawed at my heart with persistent fingers. For a while, I held her, aware but indifferent to the fact that we could be seen by anyone taking third period French.

When Hayley fell back, tears streaked her cheeks, sticking chunks of her hair to her skin. I reached out and brushed them back, tucking them with care behind her ears. She smiled at me but it was forced and sad; the sort of smile that chips away at your soul.

"They'll find her. I know it."

It wasn't much but it was all I had to offer. Blind optimism. Faith. Hope.

"What if they don't?" she murmured, her top front teeth sinking into her lip. I winced at the beads of blood that bloomed beneath the enamel.

"Don't think like that. Charlie will come back. She..."

Hayley's arm shot out, fingers sealing around my wrist underneath the sleeve of my jacket. Her grip was so tight that it was bruising and I fought the impulse to tear away from the pain.

"Olly, I think something bad happened to my sister."

"I know you're worried about Charlie, but she's smart and..."

Hayley shook her head, a growl of frustration slipping from

her pressed lips. She released my wrist and I massaged the skin, holding my arm close to my chest and out of reach.

"You don't understand." She was verging on anger. "I thought you'd get it but nobody does."

"Explain it to me."

"There's not enough time," Hayley hissed, getting so close into my personal space that her nose was almost pressed tip to tip with mine.

I couldn't step away, no matter how much I wanted to – alarmed by this sudden intensity that I'd never seen before in Hayley. She was usually cool, laid back, looking for the next joke to crack. Now, the desperation in her eyes worked like a battering ram against the shield of forced calm I'd raised. With so many other people relying on me, I'd warned myself that I couldn't afford to lose it over Charlie. Watching Hayley slowly unravel, it seemed like I'd made the right call.

Instead of retreating, I moved closer. Reaching out with both hands, I beckoned Hayley to me, urging her to accept some of the strength I was offering to lend her.

"No! I need you to listen me."

"Hayley, I can't begin to imagine what you're going through."

It was the wrong choice of words, for whatever reason. I found out, too late, when Hayley threw herself against me. She wasn't seeking comfort, though – she was looking for a punching bag, and I was unfortunate enough to be the one in reach. The blow landed on my shoulder, followed in rapid succession by a second and third. I didn't feel much of the impact due to the layers of padding in my jacket, nonetheless, the shock of the attack rocked me hard. I stumbled a step back before my senses kicked into gear and I was able to grab Hayley's wrist. Breathing fast, she glared, nostrils flaring.

"Why won't anyone listen to me? I need someone to listen!"

She choked on her plea. Shocked, I let her go and she tucked her arm into her chest as if I'd been the one hurting her. I guess I was, even if not physically.

The next words she breathed nearly swiped me off my feet.

"I have to save my sister."

I know I gaped at her. I felt my mouth drop and hang there, stuck. Catching flies, my grandma called it.

What did Hayley know that the rest of us didn't? Who exactly did she need to save Charlie from? *LostBoy666*? Some creeper on a railway platform? Herself?

Maybe it was fear of the unknown talking. Maybe not knowing where Charlie had got to was playing on the dark side of Hayley's mind. Maybe I should have been paying better attention. She was in front of me one minute and the next the door leading inside the school was swinging closed. I stared for a long time - minutes on end - until the late bell for the next period peeled. As I ran down the hall, I couldn't focus my thoughts on the Music class I was already missing. Instead of the keyboard composition piece I was writing, the notes playing on loop in my head were sinister and low: the perfect soundtrack to the horror movie my life was destined to become. I didn't know it then, of course. In retrospect, I didn't know much of anything.

All I could think of was Charlie, and how I hadn't managed to find time for her until she'd vanished without a trace.

3

DAY 2 – 16:00 HRS

I didn't expect a message from Hayley after our fight, if that's what you could call it. When my cell jingled and her name appeared at the top of the screen, I kind of expected her to be apologising for whatever had happened in the quad the day before. Instead, I received a summons that I wasn't sure how to react to.

My house. 4:30. Bring B.

Although I was kind of mad at Hayley, she was going through a lot and my conscience wouldn't allow me to ignore her. I'd successfully avoided her at school the whole day, which had made me feel bad enough. There was no way I could carry it on beyond that without a serious case of guilt plaguing me.

Without considering the alternative, I started shoving things into my purse, hoping that I'd find Hayley in a less crazy mood than I'd left her in yesterday. I was just slinging the straps of the purse onto my shoulder when my bedroom door was thrown open so wide that the handle hit the wall. I winced, wondering if the already present dent in the plaster had been deepened by the impact. Dad wouldn't exactly be excited if he had to call the housing people round to fix something else that had fallen victim to what he referred to as our 'hormonal teenage outbursts'. It wasn't as if he had to actually pay the housing company for repairs, since the military owned the every last brick and nail, but he definitely didn't enjoy listening to hold music for an hour whilst he waited for his call to connect.

"Have you seen the cars?" demanded Becca, hanging onto the doorframe with both hands as if it was holding her up.

"Sure. Metal boxes on four wheels, replaced horses and wagons."

I shooed my little sister out into the hall so I could examine the extra damage she'd inflicted on my wall. A few more snaking cracks in the plaster and a shower of magnolia flakes littering the carpet. Nothing too major. If you closed a window too vigorously in military housing then you could take out the drywall.

Becca grinned at me, eyes rolling, as I shouldered my purse and made to move past her.

"You're funny. You should do stand-up. Or you should come see the gazillion cop cars parked down the street."

My heart lurched then dropped into the pit of my stomach like a stone. I could only think of Charlie, and how the presence of more cops on base couldn't mean anything good for her. Becca must have read the worry chiselled onto my features because she stepped forward and circled an arm around my waist. I drew into her warmth, resting my head against her shoulder – made possible by the fact that she was already half a head taller than me despite being three years younger. Becca had been tall and skinny since birth, which I'll admit to teasing her about when she got on my nerves. Sometimes, to mess with her, I told her she looked like a lollipop; straight stick of a body with a giant head. She didn't actually have a giant head, but all's fair in love and sisterhood.

"Sorry, I didn't think," she murmured, voice muffled by my

hair, which she'd half pressed her face into. She pulled away when a tight coil tickled her lip.

"Let's go find out what's going on," I suggested, and we looped our arms together as we made our way downstairs.

The main yard of our house consisted of a small rectangle of neat grass, an enormous tree, and nothing else; namely, no fence or hedge to obscure our view of the neighbouring street. Every home in the five by five square was fresh from the same cookie cutter, which seemed to be how the military liked it. There wasn't one distinguishable feature among them, from the stone walls to the black shingled roofs and the matching guttering. Since Tiff's pop was a pilot, they lived over the other side of camp in the houses reserved for commissioned ranks. I could see Charlie and Hayley's house from my bedroom window. It stood on the corner of the parallel row, distinct from the others only thanks to the red, white, and blue pots that Charlie's mom had set around the step. Most people didn't bother trying to make the quarters more homely - my folks included. Dad said it seemed like a lot of trouble to go to for a space we wouldn't occupy for more than a couple of years.

Back when we'd first arrived at USAF Mildenhall, Becca and I used to hang out in the playground in the centre of the square most days. It was our only taste of freedom in this strange, foreign country, where it rained nearly every day in the summer and cars drove on the wrong side of the highway. Neither of us realised that Mom kept a near constant watch from the kitchen window.

As Becca and I jogged down the footpath laid out in front of the houses, I caught sight of a flash of blue lights from the street behind Washington Square. I picked up speed, sneakers slapping the tarmac, and Becca fell easily into step beside me with her spaghetti legs. We pushed through the gap between the corner houses and out into the street beyond in time to watch two marked police cars and a van disappear into the distance. Both of us stopped, me slightly out of breath from the jog, and Becca with one hand tangled into her hair by the roots. I had no idea how she kept her curls so neat given that they were the first thing she reached for when she felt anxious. I preferred to keep mine cropped near my shoulders, hating the extra level of upkeep when I allowed it to grow out.

"Where do you think they're going?"

I shrugged, relieved that the cars didn't seem to be stopping near the Hill's home. Directly ahead, through a small copse of trees, stood the 24 hour convenience store and gas station. Beyond it, barely out of sight, was the Exchange - a kind of colossal shopping mall where our mom worked six days a week as a deputy manager. She'd scored me the job at the ice cream parlour inside, although that was where my special privileges began and ended. I worked for my minimum wage like every other employee.

The cops seemed to have been heading in that general direction, making me wonder if some kind of trouble had started at the mall. I couldn't begin to imagine a situation that might call for so many cops. Camp was one of the safest places I could think of. Something about armed guards and barbed wire fences made most petty criminals think twice about trying their luck.

We cut through the trees, walking directly on the road in the absence of a sidewalk. It was starting to grow dark already and the air became increasingly frigid, making me regret my decision not to grab my jacket on the way out. The streetlights flickered on as the sun dipped lower and lower, but the additional light didn't untwist the knots my stomach had tied itself into. Arm in arm, Becca and I headed straight for the Exchange parking lot. We covered the distance in minutes, both searching fervently for the chaos we'd anticipated. I noticed Mom's car, parked in her usual space close to the staff entrance. However, there wasn't a single sign of trouble anywhere I looked.

"Where do you think..." Becca was interrupted by the wail of a siren. We exchanged glances - bewildered and curious - then turned to follow the din to its source.

We crossed the parking lot with increased urgency, neither one of us knowing where we were ultimately headed or what we might find once we arrived there. We walked the width of the building, past the rows of parking spaces and the line of shipping containers used for surplus storage. Eventually, the old postal service centre rose into view above the slight incline in the ground, and the mystery was solved. The redbrick building was surrounded on three sides by emergency vehicles; an overwhelming mix of police cars, military guard vans, and civilian ambulances. My hand fluttered to my mouth as the yellow crime scene tape strung around the perimeter quivered in the wind.

Uniformed cops and military personnel swarmed the site, some attempting to push back the gathering crowd whilst others focussed their attentions inside the building. The ones who flitted back and forth from inside wore plastic coverings on their shoes and stony expressions. Whatever had happened here, it wasn't good.

I recognised friends and neighbours in the throng of bodies which, every so often, surged forwards towards a temporary barrier the police had set out. Cell phones clicked and flashed as the ghouls snapped their latest *Instagram* posts.

Becca nudged me and, when I turned to her, she jerked her head to redirect my attention. Next to the back door of the mail centre, a sort of plastic tent had been erected. I'd seen that kind of thing plenty on TV and in the movies, never in real life. I knew enough to work out what the makeshift, snowy-white curtain concealed.

A body. There was a body in there.

My mouth ran so dry that my tongue felt three sizes too big, sticking to my gums as I tried to swallow. Charlie's face and the last time I'd seen it – in her bedroom, her cat settled in her lap as we listened to music – swam to the forefront of my mind. It lodged there, conjuring tears that I refused to shed until I knew the truth. It might not be her. It felt inherently wrong that I'd already started to pray that it wasn't. To keep my best friend from death, I was willing to sacrifice someone else.

"What's going on?" Becca demanded of the crowd as we shoved and wriggled our way forwards.

I caught a whiff of some guy's BO and almost tossed my cookies on my own shoes. Becca grabbed my wrist and steered me to the front, perhaps noticing how green I'd gotten. We bumped the barrier and I fell back down to earth with a jarring abruptness. My sister's fingers never loosed their grip, and I was glad of the slight pain helping to keep my head out of the clouds.

A woman I recognised from the camp diner answered. She wore her pink and purple waitress uniform, but her apron was scrunched in her hands. She wrung it out tightly, as though it was wet, before she spoke. Her eyes were troubled.

"Mail staff found a body this afternoon. Some woman who was walking her dog in the woods. The poor mutt's still running round in there, terrified. Every time someone gets close, it bolts."

"Do you know who it is?"

I blurted the question without concern for how aloof or unaffected I might sound. Charlie didn't have a dog. However, I couldn't relax until I knew who exactly was laid out beneath that tarp. There were enough people I cared about at Mildenhall to keep my gut churning up a storm.

"Kelly Pedlow," she replied, sounding a little snippier than she had seconds ago, back when she'd perceived me to be a decent person. Almost as an afterthought, the waitress crossed herself and whispered, "God rest her soul."

Becca nodded, doing a much better job of seeming like a sane, functioning member of society than I was. I brought my hand to my mouth and bit down on the tip of my thumb, embarrassed by the stinging of tears leaking from the corners of my eyes.

Mrs. Pedlow had taught me music privately since the second week I'd lived in the country. She was patient, and kind, and kept a bowl of candy on top of her practice piano to treat her students whenever they managed a particularly great lesson. Now, she was just gone.

My mind went to her beloved pet Chihuahua – Toothless – running scared through the old woods behind the postal centre whilst his owner lay dead. It wasn't the kind of place I'd want to be lost in when it got dark, even if I wasn't quite as convinced on the existence of ghosts and curses as my friends were. According to local legend, the woods at the back of camp were central to the story of Agnes Tippett. If historians and resident lunatics were to be believed, then it was where the body of the witch had been buried, and where she had died.

Years ago, Charlie, Hayley, Tiff, Rose, Becca, and I spent most of our summer in those woods, swapping scary stories and poking the ground beneath the 'twisted tree' with sticks. Hayley had climbed into its lofty branches, which stretched skyward in the shape of five gnarled fingers reaching for the clouds. It was clear from its height and spread that the 'twisted tree' was older than the tale of Agnes herself, but there was no concrete proof that her bones actually did fester beneath its roots. It was all hearsay and myth, much to Charlie's disappointment. She lapped that kind of stuff up.

"Come on, Olly, let's go."

The tug on my sleeve startled me and I whirled to find Becca watching me, concerned. I managed a nod, then I allowed myself to be guided back through the crowd and to the road we'd come from. We maintained our silence until we made it to Charlie's front door, where Becca paused with her finger hovering over the bell.

"Are you going to be okay?"

I shrugged. Probably not, I realised, but that's never the response people want to hear when they ask that kind of question.

"Mrs. Pedlow was really nice," I said, lamely.

And talented, and easy to talk to, and too young to die. I didn't add anything more, though. Whatever had happened to Mrs. Pedlow, there was nothing I could do to change it.

Becca pushed the bell and we listened as, from inside the house, the sound of three sets of footsteps filtered out into the square through the open lounge window. The door jerked inward, revealing Hayley, Tiff, and Rose - the latter looking kind of pissed off by our appearance. She crossed her arms and glared at us both, except Becca didn't notice or care as she sauntered past the girls into the hall.

"You're late." Hayley's cool tone was a good indication that she hadn't forgiven me for yesterday. I wasn't completely sure what I'd done wrong in the first place.

Irritated, I snapped back, "We were doing something important."

Hayley's eyes flashed and I knew immediately that we were in for one hell of a knock-down drag- out if one or both of us didn't back off.

"Something more important than Charlie?"

It wasn't a question, it was an indictment, but, as I was winding up to pitch my retort into her face, Becca stepped between us.

"They've found a body on camp. Mrs. Pedlow is dead."

The anger drained from Hayley's body as the colour seeped from her cheeks. She looked from Becca to me and back again as though waiting for one of us to admit to a lie. When we didn't, and the tension in the hall thickened to smothering proportions, it was Rose that took a sledgehammer to the silence.

"It was probably a heart attack. Her cholesterol had to be through the roof. She wasn't exactly bikini ready."

It was a cruel thing to say, despite the fact that Rose wasn't technically wrong. Mrs. Pedlow had her fair share of junk in her trunk. I hadn't considered her on the verge of a major coronary incident, though. She was barely middle-aged and didn't touch cigarettes or alcohol, to the best of my knowledge. So what if she liked a cheeseburger once in a while?

"Harsh," Tiff muttered under her breath, edging away from Rose as if she was scared she might catch her bitchiness through osmosis. She shot an antsy look at Hayley before she spoke again with an unusual hesitancy.

"I heard about it on my way over but I didn't want to say anything in case you were upset. Jacob Soto told me it was his mom that found the body. H-her neck was broken."

Waving away our collective shock with one hand, Rose sniffed then shrugged.

"Accident, then. She probably fell over that ratty dog of hers."

"It wasn't just broken," continued Tiff, staring at her shoes in discomfort, "Jake said her head was practically twisted all the way around. That doesn't seem much like an accident to me."

Scoffing, Rose rolled her eyes in Tiff's vicinity, her smirk implying disbelief. Then, she turned to me.

"On the bright side, Olly, Hayley, and Becca don't have to go to piano lessons anymore. Your timetables just opened right up, ladies."

She crumpled into giggles whilst Becca, Tiff, and I gaped at her – too shaken by her cold disinterest to do much else. I had probably never wanted to slap Rose Anderson more.

"Shut up, Rose."

Hayley's snarl was brutal – a surprise to us all, including Rose, whose amusement dropped away when her best friend rounded on her.

"A woman is dead and my sister is missing. How is that funny to you?"

"I didn't mean…"

"We all know what you meant," Tiff muttered under her breath, and I found myself nodding along in agreement. At my elbow, Becca held her tongue – a little more timid than me when it came to calling people out - but her anger was obvious from the tick in her jaw.

Though Rose would always tread carefully when it came to Hayley, she didn't hold the same reservations where Tiff was concerned, so she squared her shoulders and faced her judgment with haughty disdain.

"Whatever. It was a joke. If you can't take a joke then I feel sorry for you."

Tiff opened her mouth but Hayley beat her to the punch, her face tomato red and scrunched. I thought she'd been furious in the quad when she'd turned on me, however, she had reached new heights of rage listening to Rose.

"Everyone can quit it or leave," she seethed, speaking through teeth clenched tight enough to grind down to dust. "I didn't call you here so we could tear strips off of each other. If that's how you want to spend your evening then you can do it on the sidewalk, not in my house."

We all quietened, exchanging guilty glances in the wake of our telling off. The Hills were under the kind of stress that none of us wanted to imagine, so Hayley could be forgiven for her mood swings, no matter how alarming they were. If Becca was missing, I realised, I'd be grabbing collars and punching faces until someone confessed to knowing her whereabouts. I'd burn the world down for my sister.

The four of us mumbled our apologies to our shoes. They were no less sincere for lack of volume. Hayley didn't comment, stomping back upstairs without tossing out an invitation for us to join her. Unanimously, we decided we probably should, so we trailed after her with our heads bowed and our lips sealed – like naughty kids following the principal back to their office.

We crowded into Hayley's bedroom, which felt weird in itself. Usually, we congregated in the lounge downstairs to watch movies and eat snacks, or in Charlie's room if we wanted a little privacy from Mr. and Mrs. Hill. Charlie had the biggest of the three bedrooms after the master, since she was the oldest. Hayley didn't seem to mind. Her bedroom overlooked the streets behind the house, and her dad had made a padded bench to fit below the window so that she had her own reading nook. Hayley was big on reading. Three out of four of her walls were lined by bookshelves of various sizes, all filled to capacity with paperbacks, magazines, and novellas that she'd picked up over the last few years. It would be ridiculously expensive to have them all shipped back to America whenever the time came for the Hills to leave.

As Rose dropped down onto the unmade bed, she lifted a book that was spread open on the pillow and began to leaf through it. I didn't think she was really reading, more likely avoiding making eye contact with the rest of us after the incident in the hall.

The door clicked shut and Hayley sagged against the wood, head bowed, and hair falling in front of her face in thick knots. It looked like she hadn't run a brush through it for quite a while. She shoved it behind her ears without care, and I noticed how blotchy her skin looked in the artificial light. I stood around, awkward, whilst Tiff sank onto the carpet and Becca sought out the beanbag in the corner. Hayley kept her vigil at the door, taking in deep but ragged breaths – the kind that keep tears at bay. Once the others had started to squirm in their seats, Hayley came back to life.

"The week before Charlie disappeared, she wasn't acting right. Mom and Dad didn't notice but I knew something was wrong."

I froze, familiar remorse beginning to nibble at the edges of my conscience. I hadn't noticed anything wrong with Charlie in those final days because I hadn't been around. I'd picked up an extra shift or two at work, then I had a mound of assignments due in before the break, meaning what little free time was left was occupied by my music. I was planning on starting a *YouTube* channel and I'd been practicing an original song for my first upload. Mom says that when I'm absorbed in a project, I'm single-minded. I just hadn't had time left in my schedule to check in with my best friend.

"How was she acting weird?"

Tiff hugged her knees to her chest. Obviously, she hadn't noticed anything either. Our mutual failing as Charlie's friends didn't make me feel any better.

"That's not the important part," Hayley murmured, waving a hand as if to swipe away Tiff's question. She swallowed, her throat bobbing, before she continued. "The important thing is what I found. What I called you all here for."

The words that left my mouth next were the ones that sealed all of our fates. For better, for worse. Once they had been spoken, there was no taking them back.

"Show us."

4

DAY 2 – 16:56 HRS

Entering Charlie's room without her felt like a violation. Hayley had to reassure us repeatedly that her parents weren't home – out searching the neighbouring towns – before we would agree to set foot over the threshold.

When she pushed the door to herd us inside, we huddled in the middle of the room. The four of us clung together whilst Hayley groped the wall for the light switch. Almost as soon as we were washed in the blinding glow, Hayley made for the dresser. The rest of us gradually drifted apart.

Becca leaned against the doorjamb, reluctant to disturb anything. Tiff wandered off to examine the photographs pinned to the noticeboard. Needing to be helpful, I stooped down and started to gather the mix of clean and dirty clothes that covered the carpet. As the self-professed neat freak of the Hill family, Hayley's room was never in the same state of disarray as Charlie's. Despite their differences, the two of them were as close as me and Becca, and I knew Hayley had to be taking the whole situation hard. I couldn't help wondering if that meant she was searching for clues where there were none to be found.

With a cry of triumph, she slammed the dresser drawer and wheeled around with a handful of crumpled papers clutched above her head like a trophy. I set aside the blouse I'd been in the process of folding. We flocked to Hayley, bugs to a bulb, and, though I had no idea what she wanted to show us, my pulse picked up speed. Only Rose didn't approach. She bent over Charlie's vanity table, a scowl on her face.

"Why does it stink in here?"

She didn't wait on an answer before she grabbed a bottle of perfume and spritzed it into the air. A liberal shower of droplets rained down, and I felt my chest tighten as I breathed in the sickly scent. Undeniably, another odour lurked beneath; a cloying smell that I couldn't place. It was more than dried sweat and residual morning breath. Like nothing I'd experienced before.

"Probably needs airing out," said Tiff, dismissing Rose as she watched Hayley shuffle the papers. They were thrust under our noses seconds later.

I was aware of Rose grumbling, then the window opened, sending a blast of arctic air whistling into the room. Strangely, the goosebumps peppering my body had far more to do with the notes Hayley waved in my face than the October weather.

"What is this?"

"What I needed to show you. The cops barely glanced in here, so I decided to look around myself. All they cared about was the dumb cell phone."

"When did you find these?"

"Did you tell your mom and dad?"

"I don't think they'd believe me."

"You can't sit on this."

"That's why I'm showing you guys."

We all spoke at once, talking over each other, words bleeding together. Our voices rose, meshing into a high and panicked knell that kindled Rose's curiosity.

"What are you lot getting your knickers in a twist over?" The scorn in her voice matched her derisive expression. "Let me see."

Before Hayley could dodge out of reach, Rose plucked the stack from her fingers. It didn't take long for her features to slacken and her mouth to gape in disbelief. For once, she had nothing to say. It would have been a glorious moment, if it wasn't for the dark shadow looming over us.

Take out menus, sticky notes, pages torn from novels, and scraps of lined paper formed the bulk of the pile. Some were stained by coffee rings, others scrunched almost to the point beyond readability, but all with one thing in common; the word '*AGGIE*' scribbled feverishly, over and over and over, leaving barely a millimetre of paper uncovered.

"Wh-what does this mean?"

Rose rarely tripped over her words, usually so arrogant and self-assured. The change was nearly as alarming as Charlie's doodles. I stared at the *evidence*, because that was all I could think to label it in my mind. There was no obvious link between each individual page – red ink, black ink, pencil, purple marker – and no tenable explanation for the variation in her choice of canvas. It was simply as though the name had consumed her, every waking second of her days.

"What's an '*Aggie*'?"

Becca frowned as she touched a fingertip to a sushi menu. Charlie's graffiti ran over the California rolls, right through the salmon nigiri.

"Or who," suggested Tiff, taking off her glasses and rubbing the lenses on the hem of her sweater. Maybe she hoped that when she put them back on, the crazy sight in front of her would have vanished. I shuddered, wishing Rose would close the damn window and half tempted to do it myself.

"Aggie can be short for Agnes," I said, eyes flicking to Hayley. "Like Agnes Tippett."

As if to support my theory, the breeze disturbed the top page of Hayley's stack and it fluttered over, revealing a crude sketch of the 'twisted tree', completed in what appeared to be eyeliner. I heard Tiff gasp, and Rose's freckles suddenly stood out all the more as her face paled.

"No bloody way. That's a story."

Somehow, Rose didn't sound as certain as usual.

"Most stories are rooted in truth," said Tiff. "Maybe that one is, too."

"And maybe Charlie is just..." Rose started. She trailed off as she caught the flash of annoyance that crossed Hayley's face. "Maybe Charlie's not well."

I considered the idea. Charlie had always loved scary stories and horror movies - anything designed to terrify normal people. She'd been hoping that her parents would spring for us all to go on a real ghost hunt for her next birthday. She dabbled in writing - poetry and flash fiction, mostly - sometimes posting her work online in forums. That was how she'd met *LostBoy666*. He liked to create his own urban myths, she said, though she never allowed me to read one. I could have searched them online myself, I guess. It would have been easy enough since I knew his screen name, however, I hadn't thought that this boy or his stories were important enough to warrant my time.

A penchant for the paranormal wasn't exactly the mark of a crazy person, but maybe Charlie's once-endearing obsession had gone further? What if the lines between reality and fiction had started to blur, and my best friend truly believed that the monsters living in her head were coming to get her?

I couldn't help it; my gaze drifted to the posters tacked to the walls. *Pennywise* and *Leatherface* leered back at me until I had to shuffle around to turn my back to them. Their eyes continued to bore into my skull.

"There's more. Help me move the bed."

At the instruction, Tiff and I grabbed the bottom bedposts, and Hayley manned the headboard so that the three of us could swing the frame round towards the window. Becca and Rose hung back by the door, both looking equally freaked out and as if they were wondering how much weirder things could get. As we moved the bed there was dull thud, and Hayley disappeared behind the headboard for a moment, reappearing holding a half empty bottle of vodka. Shock pulsed through me and I grimaced.

"Is that Charlie's?" I planted my hands on my hips, resembling my mother when she was seconds away from losing her shit at one of us. Hayley was sheepish as she nodded.

"Yeah. I put it back when I found it on Monday. There are roll-ups in the closet, too."

"*Fruit Roll-Ups?*" asked Becca, clueless and too innocent for this world.

Hayley shook her head. The *other* kind of roll-ups, then. "She stashed them in her gym bag. Guess she knew Mom wouldn't look in there."

"Charlie wouldn't..." Tiff began, keen to leap to our friend's defence in her absence. However, she couldn't bring herself to finish the sentence in the face of the proof.

"I told you, Charlie was different. We just didn't notice in time."

The back of my neck and my cheeks grew hot, as if I was embarrassed on Charlie's behalf to be caught acting out. Cigarettes and vodka weren't exactly the worst thing a seventeen year old girl could hide, I reminded myself. Regardless, Charlie was usually a straight-A student who felt guilty if she was undercharged at the store: this wasn't like her. Except, maybe it was.

Hayley tossed the contraband onto the duvet. Clearly it wasn't the reason she'd insisted we rearrange the furniture.

"Look, right here," she ordered, crouching down on the carpet over the spot where the middle of the bed should have been positioned. "Do you see?"

Squinting, I leaned forward, trying to get a better view of the patch of carpet obscured by Hayley's shadow.

"Is that... is it blood?"

From the door, Becca spoke in a voice strangled by panic. I didn't lift my eyes from the dark, sticky stain that clung to the fibres of the carpet – turning beige to crimson in patches and splodges.

It was Tiff that answered. All I could do was stare, silenced by the nausea that had settled in my stomach.

"I don't think it's blood. See that?"

We watched in collective horror as Tiff crouched down to rub her pointer finger over the closest stain. When she withdrew her hand, she held it to the light, exhibiting a pulpy mess. She rubbed her thumb against her fingertip experimentally and a tiny seed emerged from the gunk.

"It's squished berries," she said, smiling at our gasps of relief. Without a second thought, Tiff scrubbed her fingers on her jeans, leaving a smear on her thigh.

"Like strawberries or something?"

"More like yew berries."

"Why don't you taste it and find out?" Rose suggested, her typical level of snark returning in spades now that we'd all begun to calm down.

Becca must have been feeling brave because she reached out to swat at Rose, slapping her shoulder to scold her. Whilst yew berries themselves aren't poisonous, the seeds tucked away inside can be deadly. There were signs all over Mum's Woods to warn dog walkers and parents.

"Why are there yew berries under my sister's bed? It doesn't make any sense."

I could think of at least one explanation that did. I chewed on the inside of my cheek to keep from blurting it out impulsively. Hayley was in no shape to listen to a bunch of hare brained theories, which was all I had to offer.

Tiff and Hayley pulled the bed back into position. I didn't offer to help this time. I was too absorbed in the worries spiralling around my head like a tornado. In my hand I gripped the drawing of the 'twisted tree', although I had no memory of picking it up off the duvet where Hayley had set it aside earlier. All I could focus on was the branches, spread out like fingers on a skeletal hand. Charlie had been fascinated by that tree and by the lore surrounding it.

"That's where they buried her, y'know?" she had told me, bouncing with excitement on her butt. "If you were accused of witchcraft then you couldn't be buried on holy ground."

The memory was a year old but as fresh as spring daisies.

We'd been sitting in her room, gossiping and painting our nails, a bag of chips between us, and the Hill's cat – Magic - prowling in search of attention. Eventually, he'd settled in my lap, and I'd carded my hand through his soft, snowy fur as Charlie talked.

"Mr. Friedman said that she didn't even get a trial. They just dragged her out of her house one night and into the woods. Staked her down to the ground with tree branches, right through her elbows and knees. I guess then they left her to die. How brutal is that?"

I'd shuddered, affected by the idea of some innocent teenage girl – not too unlike us – falling victim to mob justice. There was nothing about the story that appealed to me but Charlie loved a tale with a macabre ending.

"Harsh," I agreed, tickling Magic under his chin to illicit purrs.

He was Hayley's cat, really. She'd wanted a white rabbit – the kind magicians pull out of a hat – but their mom had a fear of rodents so they got a cat instead. Hayley's magic phase had ended a few months later, after the poor creature had already been named. Not that it mattered anymore. The stupid cat had up and left around a month before Charlie. Chances were he was road kill, lying in the gutter of a back road somewhere nearby, though I never said as much out loud. Hayley was kind of sensitive about it. The entire base was littered with the missing posters she'd made and copied on her lunch break at school.

I climbed out of the memory with difficulty, reluctant to let go of Charlie but unwilling to dwell on the rest of that conversation. I didn't believe in witches or curses, I reminded myself, and I sure didn't believe that Agnes had reached beyond her grave to kidnap my friend. The more I thought about it, the more likely it seemed that Charlie was either sick or in with a bad crowd she'd met on those dumb forums. I only hoped that, wherever she was, she was safe.

"You don't actually think that Charlie..." Tiff swallowed hard, steeling herself before she continued, "you don't think that Charlie was taken by an evil spirit or something?"

Nobody said a word. The silence in itself was telling. I doubted anyone truly thought that the angry spirit of an ancient witch was roaming Mildenhall to exact her revenge, but they wouldn't discount it completely, either. My friends were the type to still sleep with the closet door closed in case anything slithered out of it in the middle of the night. Becca and I had been raised with more common sense.

In the end, it was my laughter that broke the tension. The others turned their wide-eyed gazes to me - shocked by my reaction, at first - until their lips started to twitch, and they too found themselves doubled over in amusement. Only Hayley stood off to the side, solemn and with her arms folded, her downcast eyes iridescent with tears.

"I don't know what I think. I just miss my sister."

The admission sobered us like a slap. Immediately, I straightened, shame squeezing my insides. I took a step to reach out for Hayley and was a little surprised when she allowed me to drag her into my arms. She trembled against me so I held on more fiercely.

"I'm sorry. I didn't mean to laugh. That was cruel."

I felt her head shake against my shoulder and hoped that I was forgiven. The others stared at the carpet or picked at their cuticles, ashamed and uncomfortable, like me. Hayley squirmed free of my embrace after a few seconds, and I couldn't blame her. However, when she pulled back, I didn't find a trace of irritation in her gaze. Only grief.

"Thanks for coming," she mumbled, making me feel instantly more like the asshole I'd behaved as. Lately, whatever I did or said, it never seemed to be the right thing.

"I should get going. Pop is making spaghetti and I'm supposed to walk the dog before he serves up," said Tiff, smiling weakly at me over Hayley's shoulder.

Before she made for the door, she hesitated, hovering with her hands clasped to her chest as if she had something of note to say but lacked the guts for it. In the end, she settled on goodbye. I watched her go, wondering what it was that had given her pause.

Rose was next to excuse herself, muttering about homework and *Skyping* her grandma, which may or may not have been true. She forced Hayley into a tight hug that was reciprocated half-heartedly, then she dashed out the room as though the house around us was ablaze. That left Becca and me to pick up the pieces, and I could see from the twist of my sister's lips that she wasn't thrilled about it.

Becca closed the window and adjusted the curtains whilst I helped Hayley stuff the papers back into the drawer. When I found Charlie's *Smart Watch* on the windowsill, I picked it up and placed it on the nightstand without drawing attention to it. We gave the room a final cursory sweep, making sure we'd left it mostly as we found it, before we sealed it behind us again. It was a shrine, now.

Assuming we wouldn't be staying, or else tired of our company, Hayley shepherded us downstairs to the front door. I was eager to oblige, unable to spend another second in that house, where the ghost of Charlie's voice echoed from the walls. The more the hours passed, the harder it became to remind myself that she wasn't dead.

We stood on the stoop to exchange goodbyes, Hayley with her hand welded to the door handle, making it obvious that she could hardly wait to slam it in our faces. I surprised myself when I wedged my foot into the gap to hold it open a few minutes longer. I must have shocked Hayley, too, because she scowled at me like I was a door-to-door sales person or a religious zealot.

"I wanted to tell you that Becca and I are here for you. Whatever you need. Okay?"

Somehow, it didn't sound genuine, despite the fact I meant it. I wanted to look out for Charlie's little sister because, if the tables were turned, I needed to believe that someone would look out for mine. Regardless, my voice was hollow, words confusingly empty, and I was at a loss to explain the sense of detachment that ruled me. Hayley and I weren't as close as me and Charlie but we'd never been at odds, either. I chalked it up to stress and did my best to widen my smile, determined to inject the right amount of warmth into the gesture.

"Thanks," she said, eventually. She sucked on her teeth,

debating something as she watched me squirm on the step, awaiting dismissal.

"So, if you wanted to put up fliers or..."

At the snort that flew from Hayley's lips, I stopped. Anticipating trouble, Becca laid her hand on my shoulder, though whether as a supportive presence or a calming one I had no idea.

"Fliers aren't going to find my sister."

"They might," Becca countered. She managed to retain the enviably sweet tone that never failed when she was trying to get her way with our dad.

I added, more hopefully, "We could at least try. Sometimes it helps to feel like you're doing something."

"I am doing something!"

Angry Hayley was back before me suddenly – all flared nostrils and crimson cheeks. My foot fell away from the door almost subconsciously to allow for retreat. It wasn't that I was scared of her, but neither was I in a hurry to be involved in another one-sided girl fight, especially not when I was stumped by my part in the last one. A squeeze to my shoulder reminded me of Becca's presence. Straightening, I faced Hayley, determined to be patient but firm.

"We're not the enemy here, Hayley."

I was somewhat impressed by the ring of authority to my tone, though I didn't allow the mask of calm I'd perfected to slip.

"No," she murmured, swiping with her fists at the tears that flooded her eyes, "but I know who is, and you won't believe me."

The door closed with a subdued click that was so far from the resounding slam I'd been expecting that I stood motionless in shock for a while, staring at the knots in the wood. I didn't know what to make of Hayley's parting words. Was she accusing Charlie of being her own worst enemy in all of this, or was she getting at something more? Something much less believable, way beyond the bounds of what I had ever considered possible.

There were no answers to be found on the Hill's stoop, and so Becca and I made our way across the square, back home. This time, we maintained a silence that was as impenetrable as the barbed wire fences that surrounded camp.

5

DAY 2 – 19:00 HRS

Our parents hadn't seen us so downcast at dinner since Becca had failed to stick the landing in a front-handspring and was cut from the cheerleading squad for a whole six months whilst her broken collarbone knit back together.

I pushed my peas around my plate with my fork, losing any interest in eating them when they rolled through the ketchup. Most of my food remained on the plate - not untouched, since I'd chopped and played with it a good deal - but definitely uneaten. Stabbing a fry, I dunked it under the sauce until it drowned.

"Olivia, stop torturing your dinner."

Caught in the act, I looked at my mother, who arched a brow at me over the rim of her wineglass. It was a dare I wouldn't accept. I didn't back-talk my mom. She was old school, like her mama before her, and of the mind that she could easily take me out of the world she'd brought me into. I half believed she was serious about that so I picked my battles carefully, and when I could count on reinforcements.

"Sorry." I mumbled into my napkin as I dabbed my lips. It was a pantomime that I could tell my mom wasn't falling for; she hadn't seen me swallow a morsel of food. However, her stare was more concerned than challenging. She already knew what was on my mind.

"Is there an update on Charlie?"

She set down her wine and the clink of cheap glass on wood was almost musical. I watched the ruby red liquid slosh around the belly of the glass - high enough to kiss the lip on both sides - finding it so hypnotic that I only glanced up again when Mom cleared her throat. I shook my head in reply to her question, which was one I was getting tired of answering. Half the students in school, plus some of the teachers, seemed to think I was the font of all knowledge when it came to Charlie's disappearance. I'd been hounded relentlessly all day for news that I didn't have.

"If you want to talk, Dad and I are here," she reminded me, pitying.

It was easy to forget sometimes that our parents had forged friendships of their own. Mom and Mrs. Hill were close enough that they had regular movie nights and went Christmas shopping together. She probably would have asked Carolyn Hill about Charlie herself but, one lasagne and two casseroles on the doorstep later, she was unresponsive to Mom's calls. We figured she was pouring all of her time into the search for her daughter, understandably. Nonetheless, I could tell that Mom was sensitive about it. Whilst I'd lost a friend, it probably felt to Mom like the same was happening to her, especially since Mrs. Hill was batting away her best attempts at being supportive.

We continued dinner in silence, only now it wasn't just me pushing food round their plate. Mom's fork squealed against the china as she prodded her chicken and, her hypocrisy noted, she flashed me a smirk.

"I know it's not the best time to bring this up," Dad cut in, laying down his cutlery and levelling the three of us with the most serious expression in his arsenal, "but I want everyone to stay away from Mum's Woods for a while."

Becca's knife clattered from her grasp to strike her plate but nobody looked away from Dad. Tension mounted in our dining room until it was solid enough to climb like a ladder. I knew I couldn't be the only one whose heart was slamming painfully against their ribcage. Just the mention of those woods suddenly had that effect on me.

"Is this about Mrs. Pedlow?"

Dad's eyes flashed to Becca in alarm, and I could see the cogs whirring in his mind as he tried to work out how much my sister might know on the subject.

"Do the police know what happened?" Mom demanded before Dad could answer Becca.

I watched him wipe an imaginary spot of sauce from his chin with his napkin to buy himself extra time. He laid his knife and fork in the centre of his plate, and it became obvious that none of us were going to be finishing our food.

"Some kind of freak accident. Poor woman."

"She was such a sweet lady," Mom echoed, and she tipped her glass to the ceiling in tribute before she took another sip.

"I don't want you girls to be scared, but I'd prefer you stay away from the place for a spell. Out of respect."

Mom nodded in agreement and Dad lowered his head over his abandoned meal. The bulbs in the dining room chandelier burned bright and the light they threw out refracted off Dad's burgeoning bald spot. It was nearly enough to dazzle if you looked straight at it. When I turned away, it had nothing to do with the glare from Dad's head. Although I wanted to be, I wasn't convinced by his explanation. Neither was Becca, judging by her crossed arms and creased brow. How could a woman's head be *accidentally* twisted all the way round? It shouldn't be physically possible. But, then, I supposed I wasn't an authority on that kind of thing. Regardless, I wasn't going to argue against Dad's wishes when Mum's Woods wasn't among my favourite hangout spots anymore. Sure, it was peaceful there, and the trees were good for climbing when I was young enough to be into that kind of thing. However, as I'd grown older, I'd noticed more and more the small details that made others shy away from the spot behind the old post office; how the air felt smothering, oppressive and difficult to breathe, and how the sound of birdsong faded into oblivion the closer you drew to the heart.

"Don't you think it's weird timing? A disappearance and a murder all in the same week? It's not like anything bad ever usually happens at Mildenhall."

I cringed, listening to Becca lay it out so starkly. Across the table, Mom's eye twitched and I could see that she wasn't unaffected by Becca's candour. Dad, meanwhile, took it all in his stride, as usual.

"It's not been an easy week, that's for sure," he admonished, "but the two things aren't related, Bec. What happened to Mrs. Pedlow is a tragedy."

My ears pricked up and I waited for him to continue, holding my breath. If he had some kind of opinion to offer on Charlie then I was keen to hear it. Out of all the adults in my life, I trusted my father perhaps the most to examine things with a level head. He was a military man through and through, having grown up like Becca and me as a camp brat. Mom often joked that he didn't just bleed red but also white and blue. So much time spent in service had forged a logical man with an analytical mind who was good in a crisis. Dad was definitely the guy to have on your team, no matter what the game.

"I know that this business with Charlie has hit you both hard, and I'm so sorry this has happened. But I don't think we can overlook the evidence, here. The most likely explanation is that Charlie has run away. Now, I hope, in time, she'll realise her mistake and come home, but until then, the most we can do is be there for her family, and pray."

Loading the dishwasher was my job – one I'd completed hundreds of times since moving into our quarter – yet that night I couldn't make the plates and glasses fit no matter how many times I rearranged them. In the end, when the clattering bordered on violent, Mom shooed me upstairs so she could pick up my slack. I had a mountain of homework to focus on, plus piano practice, but my brain refused to process any of it. Instead, it tormented me, playing past memories of Charlie on loop until I kind of wished I'd borrowed that half bottle of vodka from her bedroom. Anything to silence my thoughts.

I hid away in my room until it was time for bed. It had become habit for Becca and me to share the bathroom in the evening, so it wasn't unexpected when I found her waiting for me in the hall at ten on the nose, arms full of supplies. Becca used her teeth to grip the dangling light cord and give it a tug. Mom was always warning her against that, scared that she'd break her perfect teeth or something, but Becca never listened.

For a while, we focussed on the familiar: wiping off our makeup, exfoliating, moisturising, squeezing occasional blackheads. It was as Becca was tucking her hair away underneath the silk cap she wore to bed that she focussed her eyes on me through the mirror. I was in the middle of flossing, the string hanging out of my mouth from the slight gap between by front teeth. I stared back at my sister through the glass, expectant.

"Do you think Charlie ran away?"

The floss snagged on my gum and I winced, drawing it out before tossing it into the open toilet and spitting blood into the sink.

"She met a guy online. Who knows?"

"I thought you knew," Becca accused, back to folding her arms and scowling at me. Her socked foot tapped against the linoleum; a rhythm of frustration. "You know Charlie better than any of us. Is running away with some internet guy something you actually think she'd do?"

I turned on the faucet, washing away the remnants of my overzealous flossing with a torrent of water. Then, I leaned over the sink and filled one of the disposable cups that Mom kept on the shelf below the mirror. The plastic buckled and bent in my hand, malleable to the barest tightening of my fingers. I eased my grip before I sloshed water all over the floor, and set it on the counter.

"Maybe I didn't know Charlie as well as we all thought."

I tried for nonchalant. Instead, I sounded heartbroken. Taking a step forward, Becca rested a hand on my shoulder. That frown she had been wearing for the better part of five days evaporated under the heat of the bathroom light. Her eyes watered but she didn't cry. We'd done enough of that already.

"None of this is your fault. Nobody thinks that."

I did. I thought that, I realised, with a stab of remorse to my gut that nearly doubled me over.

"I should have been there for her." The words caught at the back of my throat, suffocating. "I've been too busy thinking about myself, my music, my assignments. I didn't make time for Charlie... now she's gone."

"Oh Olly."

Becca surged forwards and I met her halfway, my body aching for the reassurance of my sister's arms. We pressed together, exhausted by the burden of the last few days and both trembling from the cold of the bathroom. Burying my nose in my sister's shoulder, I breathed in the scent of her hair oil, relying on the familiarity for comfort.

"I should have been a better friend."

"Whatever Charlie does is on her. You aren't responsible for other people's choices. You get that, right?"

Becca untangled herself from me, holding me by the shoulders at arm's length so that she could pin me in place. I bowed my head to shirk her glare and she shook me a little to let me know my evasiveness hadn't escaped her.

I wasn't certain I could believe what she said. She was my sister and there was no way she'd lay blame at my feet for something as serious as this. Her judgment was skewed when it came down to it: I was as aware of that fact as I was of how epically I'd let my friend down. Maybe all Charlie had needed was a sounding board – someone to talk to about whatever crap *LostBoy666* had filled her head with. I would have been that for her once, unquestionably. Before I'd become so self-absorbed that I'd shut her out. With nowhere to turn, had she turned away instead? Or had she been duped by some psycho guy into abandoning the life she'd always known?

When I realised that Becca was waiting on a response, I managed to nod my head to satisfy her. She was no fool, and my distress was obvious, but there was nothing more my sister could add that would help in any way. Knowing this, she leaned forward to kiss my cheek.

"You're not selfish," she promised, tugging on one of my wayward curls then watching it spring half-heartedly back towards my ears. "You're just really shit at hair care."

I giggled, even though I didn't want to, and Becca cracked a smile that made the apples of her cheeks shine.

"Thank you, I appreciate your honesty."

"Any time, sis," she replied, before she swept her lotions and potions back into her comically enormous cosmetic bag. She shifted it into her arms and wedged the bulk against her body with the right one, leaving the left free for all kinds of trouble. Lingering at the door, Becca mocked a salute that would have made Dad wince, and followed by flipping me off with the same hand.

A snort made it past my lips and I looked away fast to avoid encouraging her. She wouldn't have dared to play like that if Mom and Dad had been around, but apparently the hum of the TV from downstairs was enough to assure her that she wouldn't be busted.

"Go to bed!" I directed, between the laughter I muffled with the back of my hand and shaking my head in despair. At least I could count on my sister to cheer me up when things went south.

I listened to her shuffle down the hall to her bedroom, dragging her feet – the friction of fluffy socks on carpet setting my teeth on edge. It was my personal equivalent to the dentist's drill or speaker feedback. Becca knew that and she did it all the more to irritate me. I'd get my revenge on her tomorrow, when I could swap out the sugar in her coffee for salt. We liked to mess with each other, although there was no malice in it. It had become another way of showing our affection.

As Becca's door closed, I shoved zit cream and moisturiser back into my wash bag. I took a second to evaluate the state of my hair in the mirror, wincing at the static mess. Once-defined curls had started to resemble an amorphous cloud. For sure, Becca hadn't been wrong about me neglecting my hair. For the briefest moment, I considered calling her back - begging her to teach me her ways and save me from the inevitable puffiness. In the end, I decided I would spray my head with water in the morning and hope for the best, like I did every other day. With my bag nestled under my arm, I reached for my cup and turned to leave the bathroom.

Looking back, I couldn't possibly identify what it was that stopped me in my tracks. Everything appeared so normal. There were no insidious noises, no looming presences or phantom odours of rot, and absolutely no other clichés to chill the blood that rushed through my veins. There was simply that feeling you sometimes get when you are forced to question how alone you truly are in a vacant room. One by one by one, the fine hairs on the nape of my neck stood to attention. I waited for the sensation of icy breath on my skin with my stomach clenching and my leg muscles coiling in preparation to run. When nothing happened, there was relief and also confusion, and I whipped around to see what the hold-up was. I found the space behind me empty, shower curtain pulled open to expose the tub. Despite this, the feeling of unease lingered and snowballed until my breath was coming in rasps that made me sound asthmatic. Realisation took me over second by second and, horrified, I knew both where I should direct my gaze and exactly what I would find there. Those movies I watched all the time with Charlie had primed me for it; the spectre in the mirror, blood welling from the eyes, talons scraping in a frantic bid to break through the glass. The tattered, white dress would be a given. I didn't know how or why – it wasn't like I'd played the *Bloody Mary* game since third grade – still, I knew it with confidence. I only had to steal myself to face it.

Ripping off the band aid, I twisted around, almost dropping my wash bag in my hurry to meet my fate. I stared into the mirror, doe-eyed and gasping. My own panicked reflection looked back.

A laugh burbled from my chest. Gradually, the hairs that lined up on parade on the back of my neck calmed and lay back down. Warmth returned to my body in a rush - aided by embarrassment at my own immaturity - and my heart shook off the palpitations that had plagued it. *Idiot.*

My breathing on the cusp of normal, I set my bag on the counter and raised my cup to take a steadying sip. Over the plastic lip, the surface of the water rippled. A single bubble rose from the depths to pop on the surface and I ignored it so I could drink deep. Savouring the coolness, I held the water in my mouth for a while before I swallowed. I felt better, less shaky, more rational, and ready to sink into my mattress to try for at least a few hours of sleep. I stretched for my cosmetic bag, and that was when I noticed it: inside the cup, the water had begun to undulate, as if stirred by an invisible finger.

I drew the beaker to eye level to investigate, so close that the tip of my nose brushed the side. It pressed a shallow dip into the plastic. The ripples grew in intensity without warning, swelling larger and coming more frequently. Water rocked back and forth in the tumbler at a violent pace, stirred by a wind that didn't exist. I didn't move - didn't breathe - didn't think. I couldn't.

Stillness returned to the glass, making me consider the possibility that I'd imagined the whole thing. It was then, as I was recovering my breath, that the water inexplicably clouded, confirming that I had not.

Through the murk, I picked out an image in vibrant colour; pale yet freckle dappled skin; long auburn hair; a silver star-shaped nose-stud that winked when the light hit it.

Charlie.

The picture of my best friend was clear. Undeniable. It was Charlie, alright, as I remembered her, in perfect detail. Reflected in my water beaker.

I blinked, frantically, and blinked again when the impossible didn't clear from my vision. Charlie watched me, her nostrils flaring on both sides. I realised she was crying, though it was difficult to tell with her tears being lost to the water.

"Charlie," I croaked in a hoarse tone that shredded my vocal cords on the way out. "*Charlie*. Charlie, where are you?"

If she heard me at all, she chose not to respond. That hurt as much as being told she had disappeared.

"Let me help you," I beseeched her, looking into the cup. I didn't stop to contemplate how I'd embraced the improbable so quickly in my desperation. It seemed natural, yet it was anything but.

I opened my mouth to plead with her once more – this spectre of my friend – but no words made it past my lips. Charlie met my gaze and, so suddenly that I couldn't pre-empt it, she threw back her head and howled.

It rang in my ears and in my mind, ricocheting through the hollows in my bones until my teeth vibrated. The sound was mournful and deafening, and it blared from Charlie for longer than should have been humanly possible. From experience I knew that people could hold notes for a finite time. I clawed at the idea that she would need to breathe soon. She didn't.

Fright got the better of me before my eardrums could rupture from the pressure. I crushed the cup, mangling it in my fist, and the water flooded over the rim to soak my ankles and the tiles under my feet. A puddle gathered but I didn't care. Charlie's scream haunted my ears, making them pound inside as aggressively as my heart.

Dropping the beaker, I ran from the bathroom – not stopping to grab my bag or turn off the light, and definitely not to clear up my mess. I made for my bedroom, socks sliding, sending me skidding into the hall so that I barely had time to latch onto the frame.

I wouldn't look back. I didn't want to know if Charlie's image remained, transferred to the tile, beneath the blur of the bathroom light and the hum of the ceiling fan. It was too much. If this was the by-product of a guilty conscience then I had to find some way to fix it, fast.

Before I wound up lost, like Charlie.

6

DAY 3 – 18:00 HRS

Purple ice cream, melting in the heat of the mall, dribbled down my thumb to pool on the counter. I resisted the urge to pop the digit into my mouth and suck it clean. I doubted Tiff, as my only customer, would have minded, but at least one security camera was trained on me, and that was definitely the kind of conduct my boss frowned on.

"Sprinkles or sauce?" After all this time, it wasn't like I had to ask. I did anyway. I wasn't firing on all cylinders and the small talk cajoled my brain into a state of semi-functioning. Tiff grinned at me as she reached for the pot of chocolate flakes beside the register. I pulled it away from her, ignoring the crestfallen expression and pout I earned.

"No more freebies," I scolded. "Mr. Maroney is on my back after the last stock take. I can't keep pretending I'm dropping things."

It was the truth. Following his stock check - plus two packets of MIA fudge sticks, a box of flakes, and a tub of Bubblegum Blast - Maroney had vowed to make me pay out of my wages for anything I wrote in the wastage book. He wasn't a man to make idle threats so I'd decided it was time to cut my friends off from their frozen treat dependency before Mr. Maroney cut me off from gainful employment.

"I'll pay."

Tiff beamed when I rolled my eyes then shoved the pot back in her direction. She grabbed two flakes and stuck both in her mouth at once, her eyes bulging from the sockets as she mimed walrus tusks. When I didn't laugh, she took offence and yanked the flakes from her mouth to stuff into the top of her cone. A blob of blueberry cheesecake ice cream landed on her napkin and I stared at it for longer than was socially acceptable. Before I knew it, Tiff was waving her hand in front of my eyes, demanding my attention, which had admittedly been wandering all day. I couldn't stop thinking about what had happened in the bathroom. The water. Charlie's face. That scream. She had sounded wounded, like she'd been set alight and left to burn. I shivered at the idea and reached for the raspberry sauce bottle to complete Tiff's order.

"Did you sleep at all last night?"

As if my haunted raccoon eyes weren't answer enough. I stared at her dumbly, wondering what she'd say if I were to tell her. After Charlie's scribbles and sketches, she'd probably worry that insanity was contagious. I debated for a second if it might be, then shoved the thought away when I realised there was no merit in it. *Focus on the problems you have,* Dad would say, *not the ones that might be waiting round the corner.*

"I'll try get an early night tonight," I replied, finally, squirting out sauce with a loud slurp. Tiff looked up in surprise from chewing on her spoon. I guess she had forgotten I was even there thanks to my uncharacteristic silence.

"What's the damage?" she said, lodging the spoon in her ice cream and digging around in her purse for her wallet. I hit a few extra buttons, adding on the sauce and second flake. There was no way Maroney would catch me out.

Gesturing to the customer display on the register, I focussed on cleaning my spills whilst Tiff fumbled. When she eventually pulled her hand from the depths of her purse, she did so with a gust of laughter. She opened her clenched fist, scattering a dozen or so tiny, red balls across the surface of the counter. Automatically, my hand shot out as a couple rolled towards the edge. I plucked them up with my thumb and index finger, holding them to the light with curiosity. Yew berries.

My shudder was so deep that I was surprised Tiff didn't hear my brain rattle with it. A sideways glance told me she'd hardly noticed my reaction at all, too busy bent double as she giggled over the find. I didn't see anything funny about it. Had she so quickly forgotten Charlie's room? The discovery under the bed?

Before I could remind her, Tiff had swept the berries back into her sky-blue, furry purse and tapped her debit card to the reader. The sale processed with the automatic ching-ching that I'd loved when I first started at the parlour, but had come to loathe after a solid summer of serving ice cream to every man, woman, child, and canine stationed at RAF Mildenhall.

"I walked the dogs before I came here. Must have brushed past a tree or something," she said, her casual lack of concern a far more normal reaction than the sudden panic that spiked through me.

"My dad says we should all stay away from the woods."

I blurted the warning out on impulse. Tiff focussed an odd, narrow-eyed gaze on me, and I strangled the cloth in my hand. She shouldered her bag. I continued to stare at it as though it had personally offended me – beyond being a crime against fashion.

"Is this about Mrs. Pedlow? Pop says she didn't die in the woods. Plus, it was an accident, anyway."

All I could manage was a nod. Dissatisfied, Tiff continued,

and I gripped the cloth harder so that residual cleaning fluid leeched out onto my hand.

"Trust me, the scariest thing about those woods is the prospect of catching Riley Simmons with her tongue in the next poor, unsuspecting guy's mouth."

She wasn't wrong on that score. Riley changed her boyfriend more times in a week than I changed my jeans. It wasn't that I was trying to slut shame her or anything, since that's just gross misogyny, but Riley was the worst. She was the kind of girl who hated everybody without a Y chromosome and a car, and wasn't shy about conveying it.

"I guess that's true." I eased up on the cloth before tossing it into the laundry bin next to the counter.

"Definitely," confirmed Tiff, with a belated smirk, before she added, "unless you do believe all those stories about the ghost of Agnes Tippett?"

Maybe I had once, back when we'd first arrived at Mildenhall, and Charlie had regaled us with the tale of the Mum's witch whilst we stared at the deformed branches of the 'twisted tree'. Aggie Tippett had been buried beneath the roots of that monstrosity, so Charlie insisted - her evil poisoning the ground until the tree itself suffered for it.

"Some people think that you can call the witch back, if you know how. But she'll be angry and mean, and it'll cost you seven souls. The witch is always looking for souls to trade with the devil for her freedom," Charlie had revealed, watching in poorly disguised delight as Hayley and Becca had shuffled closer to me.

When I thought about it, Charlie had always been strange, even when we were kids. It was unnerving to most adults, who considered her way too macabre for a child, but it had been one of the things that had drawn me to Charlie most; her determination to unapologetically be herself.

"Of course I don't," I said, chuckling at Tiff to hide my discomfort.

There were so many memories of Charlie recently that clamoured to reach the front of my mind, and I had begun to despise them all. Being reminded of what you've lost sometimes hurts more than losing it in the first place. The thing that proved hardest to push away, however, was the image of her face in the tumbler.

"Do you think people can see things... when they're stressed and stuff?"

It came out wrong, not at all how I'd rehearsed it in my head, so I forced a smile to cover for my nerves.

"What kind of things?"

Thankfully, Tiff kept her eyes on her cone as she spun it deftly in one hand so that she could lap at the edges. The centre of her tongue, which became visible with each lick, had started to turn mauve.

"I don't know." I shrugged, then buried my hands in the front pocket of my apron. "Things that aren't really there."

She stilled, mid-lick, her tongue buried in the ice cream so deep that I started to wonder if the temperature had it stuck there. After a few moments, she drew it back into her mouth, negating my concern.

"When my Aunt Kayla died a couple of years back, my uncle swore he saw her afterwards, in the garden, pruning their rose bushes. Happened every Tuesday like clockwork for six months. As soon as he'd run out to talk to her, she'd disappear."

Tiff let out a gentle breath and her eyes clouded with the mist of grief.

"Tuesday had always been her day to garden. Uncle Jack would get home from work and Kayla would be out there in her dungarees with her huge, floppy hat, elbow deep in mud and cuttings. It was her favourite place in the world to be."

It was a sad story but I found myself enchanted by it. I clung on to not only the words but to every individual syllable, like they were something precious.

"What happened?" I probed when Tiff didn't seem like she was going to be forthcoming with more information.

"Uncle Jack had a breakdown at work. After a few months on meds, he was doing okay. Never saw Kayla again after that."

Not exactly the news I'd been hoping for. I didn't have either the time or inclination for a breakdown. All I really wanted was to find Charlie and draw a line under the ordeal. On the other hand, Uncle Jack's story went at least some ways in proving that the mind was capable of conjuring all sorts of impossibilities under pressure. How different was a dead woman pruning her rose bushes to a missing girl in a water cup? They could be one and the same, I promised myself.

"So, it's a real 'thing', then?"

Tiff wiped a smear of ice cream from the tip of her nose as she nodded at me. When she'd finished with the napkin, she didn't push it aside, she moved it into her lap where she could better manipulate each tuck and fold.

"Yep. Totally. I've seen it on TV." Her hands worked overtime, flying with such speed that I couldn't keep track of their work. *Well*, I thought sardonically, *how could I argue with TV?*

"I have to shoot, I'm sitting for the Mirandas in an hour," said Tiff as she slid off her stool, dragging her purse with her by the strap. I shook my head, biting my lip to stave off a grin at her bag, which looked a lot like she'd skinned *Miss. Piggy's* ex-boyfriend. Tiff definitely walked on the wilder side when it came to her wardrobe choices. She had an eye for vintage and handmade clothing, and a knack for matching patterns that I would never in a billion years have expected to look cute together. If I'd allowed it, she and Becca would have paired up at a moment's notice to give me the mother of all makeovers.

Tiff wiped her hands clean with a second napkin, which she balled then tossed at the garbage. She missed by wide inches and I laughed at her misfortune, like only a true friend would. The first napkin found its way onto the counter. Tiff had managed to fold it into a tiny origami ghost, and I realised that the last laugh was going to be hers. She grinned cheekily as she dodged the cloth I swung into her face.

"Adorable," I said, hiding my amusement poorly. I crushed *Casper* under my fist and Tiff blew me a kiss as she sauntered away towards the exit.

After she left the parlour, the rest of my shift passed as painfully as getting my braces tightened. Although the BX Exchange always had plenty of customers, there was never much demand for ice cream during a British winter. If it wasn't for all the chocolate flakes they talked me into slipping them, my friends would probably have been credited with single-handedly keeping the place open from September through to April. Most people who wandered into the mall during the cold season were looking for a tax-free couch or the latest *Kindle*, rather than a triple scoop sundae. They could find both at the Exchange, along with everything from kids' toys to sporting equipment to barbecues. Not that anyone needed one of those in England in October. You were lucky if you needed one in the middle of July some years.

Occasionally, I missed Colorado, but I mostly kept that to myself. I knew I was fortunate to be able to see the world at a young age, when I didn't have to worry about the costs that came with emigration. Even though I didn't think I could ever settle in Britain for real, it was a cool experience to live in another country for a while - especially one that wasn't too dissimilar to where I'd come from. The people were friendly, for the most part, and the food was good, if you didn't count blood pudding or trifle. Not to mention, I'd never quite recovered from the awe I felt the first time I visited an honest-to-God castle.

Walking home alone in the dark had never unnerved me before that night. The guards usually drove around camp every hour on patrol, so I had always felt like there was someone looking out for me. With Mrs. Pedlow's accident, and probably Charlie's disappearance, the patrols had been doubled down on. Despite this, I found myself looking over my shoulder every second step until I reached Washington Square and the edge of our front lawn came into view in the distance. I ran the rest of the way, grateful when Becca swung the door open - as though she'd been waiting for me at the window – so I didn't have to fumble for my keys.

Mom and Dad had gone out for date night, and Becca had already ordered pizza in my absence. She'd at least been decent enough to wait for me to get home before she'd attacked the box, although she had ordered extra pineapple, so that was where my gratitude ended. We loaded slices onto paper plates we'd found in the kitchen drawer, congratulating ourselves on avoiding dish washer duty, then we took our food to the lounge.

I was distracted with flicking slimy chunks of pineapple off my dinner when my cell rang. Becca looked away from the TV, pausing in her task of flipping between channels at a rate of knots as she waited to see who was calling me after nine on a school night. Our parents were strict about cell phones. On weekdays we were expected to hand them over at ten. We got them back in the morning before we left for school, much to Becca's annoyance. Whoever was calling me either wasn't aware of the rules or else was open to playing fast and loose with them. Just for a second, I wondered if it could be Charlie, trying to reach out from wherever she was hiding. Or maybe being held. I set my plate on the couch with renewed urgency, forgetting that the grease would bleed right through the paper to stain the cushions. Mom would be furious.

I grabbed my phone from my jacket pocket so fast that it almost slid out of my hand but I managed to hold onto it somehow. My eyes focussed in on the caller ID photo flashing onscreen. It was Tiff's face - not Charlie's - that beamed back, and I tried not to dwell on the disappointment swelling in my chest like an inflating balloon.

It was a great photo of Tiff, really. The green streaks she'd threaded through her hair in spring were vivid against the dark backdrop of her shirt. The colour made her eyes pop, with their shades of hazel and emerald married together. However, hers hadn't been the face I'd been hoping to see at all. Working hard to keep the frustration from my voice, I answered on the sixth ring.

"Kids being pains in your ass? I can't come over and save you right now. Mom and Dad will..."

There wasn't a chance to finish. A sob – loud and anguished, almost verging on a wail – erupted through the line. A sniffle followed, then there was only overwhelming silence.

"Tiff?" When I received no response, I demanded more desperately, "Tiffany? Are you okay?"

Becca turned off the TV and slid her plate onto the floor. She shuffled over to me on her knees, her wide eyes asking questions I had no answers for.

"If this is a joke then it's not funny. Answer me right now or I'm hanging up and calling the cops."

Though I could detect the hiss of steady breathing on the line, I wasn't reassured. My stomach lurched and I wondered how long I'd be able to hold onto the slice of pizza I'd eaten if Tiff didn't say something.

"Please talk to me," I begged, one last ditch attempt, as my guts cramped in warning.

There was a deep breath, proceeded by a whisper - far too high and sweetly innocent. Not my friend yet vaguely familiar for reasons I couldn't pinpoint. A child, I realised, with panic wavering inside me. The line snap, crackled, and popped, before that little voice felled me with a single swing.

"Tiffy's gone."

7

DAY 3 – 21:40 HRS

The Miranda house was less than a ten minute walk away from Washington Square. It was the first on its block, sitting directly behind the library, and I knew it well since Tiff had been babysitting for the family for over a year. Sometimes I went with her, although I never took a cut of her money when she offered. The kids were sweet and I didn't mind keeping Tiff company since she did the same for me on slow days at the parlour. This time, though, I didn't walk there: I sprinted.

The call had disconnected moments after tiny Ramona Miranda had uttered her tearful statement. I'd been in motion before I'd fully digested what she'd said. Becca followed as I garbled an explanation. She zipped her jacket to her chin and slid the hood over her head whilst I hunted for my keys. It had started to rain and the sidewalks were already slick with it. I realised, too late, that I'd forgotten to change out of my house shoes into my sneakers. They were soaked through before I made it to the next street but I didn't dare to turn back to fix my mistake. Ramona was only five years old – her sister, Sara, in diapers – and I didn't want to contemplate what might happen if the kids truly had been left. It didn't sound like something Tiff would do, but I'd been wrong about my friends before. I prayed that Ramona was playing some kind of game that she was simply too young to understand the consequences of.

Somehow, Becca had known where to turn off, and she'd reached the Miranda house ahead of me. She was already banging on the front door with both fists when I barrelled round the corner, breathless, windswept, and looking crazy in a pair of *Yoda* slippers. Ignoring how my socks clung to the soles of my feet, like another layer of skin, I joined Becca on the stoop to peer in through the front door glass. She continued to knock as I pressed my face to the pane and cupped my hands around my eyes to block out the streetlights. The hall beyond was dark and I saw nothing either alarming or reassuring. In fact, I saw nothing at all.

Becca, who had been leaning on the doorbell with the palm of her hand, shot me a look of rising alarm. There was something wrong here. We had been making enough noise to rouse the dead yet nobody had shuffled into view to answer the door or tell us to quit with the racket.

"All the kid said was that Tiff was gone?" she checked. "She didn't say where? Like, gone to the store or..."

"Tiff wouldn't be so irresponsible," I snapped, too chewed up by desperation to feel bad for lashing out.

Nodding, Becca jammed her hands into her jacket pockets and leaned back on the steps to allow herself a better view of the street. At the adjacent house, a cat pawed at a window, demanding to be let in. Nothing else stirred in the darkness except for us.

"We could go round back?"

It was the only solution left, aside from making good on my threat of phoning the cops. However, I didn't want to risk doing that too soon and end up embarrassed if it turned out that Ramona *was* pulling a prank behind Tiff's back. I doubted the Mirandas would be impressed if they came home to find squad cars in their drive and the cops reading their babysitter the riot act. Tiff wouldn't be much impressed, either. Maybe she had her earbuds in. Maybe her music was turned up so loud that it drowned out everything else, like the pounding on the door and a little girl making crank calls. That had to be it.

We circled round to the backyard. Becca made better headway than me in my soggy house shoes, which squelched into the grass. It was getting harder and harder to lift my feet but I kept on, letting my anxiety drive me more than the rain and the cold could.

"The fence is pretty low. We should be able to climb over it," said Becca. She yanked down her hood, sacrificing her hair to the elements, so that she could get a better look at the fence.

I left her scrabbling for a foothold and walked further along the perimeter to check if there was a gate. There wasn't, I discovered, but one of wooden panels had splintered and snapped completely in half - probably the victim of a recent storm. Seizing the opportunity it presented me, I hopped over, grateful that I didn't have to scale anything in my *Yodas*.

I touched down in the flower border and had to fight my way through a bush before I managed to reach the lawn. Ahead, the kitchen light burned - the only one in the entire house. Every other window radiated darkness, and I shivered as I stared for a few seconds longer.

"How did you beat me over?"

My sister was at my side, glowering over the fact I had conquered the fence before her. There wasn't a single athletic bone in my body and we both knew it. In contrast, Becca had won so many medals and trophies that she'd run out of wall space to display them. If it hadn't been a potential emergency then I would have teased her over her pettiness.

"Fence is broken." I jerked a thumb at the gap.

Becca's eyes ticked to the damage and the lines at the corners of her mouth deepened with her frown. It looked like something large and heavy had careered into the panel, but Mom was always saying that wind damage was no joke.

"Let's go," I insisted, tugging on Becca's sleeve.

We had walked no more than a few paces towards the screen door when my foot landed on a foreign object. I yelped as something sharp bit through the sole of my house shoe. Whatever it was, I could feel it sinking into the mud with my weight bearing down on it. Using her cell phone as a torch, Becca stooped to retrieve the object whilst I hopped around on my uninjured foot, waiting for the niggling pain to fade from the other.

"Crap."

Becca's curse was enough to freeze me on the spot - one leg in the air and arms out at my sides for balance. With her torch pointed at her palm, Becca thrust her hand under my nose so that I could get a good look at whatever I'd stepped on. It was a pair of glasses. One of the arms was missing, and dirty rainwater ran off them in rivulets, but the lenses were intact inside the chunky, green plastic frames. They were Tiff's glasses, without a doubt. She had been so pleased with them a few months back after she'd talked her dads into springing for designer frames. They'd decided she was finally mature enough to respect the expense, and Tiff had treated those glasses as if they were made of gold. Now, here they were, abandoned in the filth without their owner. Becca folded the glasses as best she could, considering the damage, and shoved them into her back pocket. I limped towards the house with renewed resolve, certain that I wasn't going to like what I would find inside.

With my hand on the handle, I whispered a prayer under my

breath before I tested the door to check if it was unlocked. It slid open with a shushing sound that was music to my ears. Behind me, Becca was eager to get out of the driving rain and so she prodded me in the back to encourage me into the kitchen. I stumbled over the raised runner, barely managing to correct myself without grabbing onto the counter. Right-*Yoda* and left-*Yoda* slapped the linoleum, leaving wet prints in my wake.

A scan of the room revealed a sink full of dishes, and colouring books with crayons scattered across the table. A half empty bottle of formula stood next to a baby monitor unit, which I assumed was turned on since it winked alternate green and red. I looked around frantically for signs of life – Tiff, one of the children, even a wandering pet – but I saw none. There was that feeling again, though, as if I was being watched from nearby, and I slammed the screen door shut behind us to dispel it.

"Tiffany! You here?" Becca yelled. I startled - my hand over my heart - having forgotten that I had a voice to make use of.

"Tiff?" I joined in Becca's calls, and we moved from room to room downstairs, eager for a reply.

Dining room, laundry room, lounge, shower room; none of them yielded any results, and I was starting to become frenzied as I dashed around in search of my friend. We switched on every light as we went so we didn't miss anything important, but the absence of shadows didn't calm me. Becca dug her phone out of her pocket once more and tried calling Tiff. She waited with her hand on her hip and her bottom lip between her teeth whilst I wore a trench in the lounge floor with my pacing. My ears pricked up when the *Scooby Doo* theme filtered weakly into the room. We followed the music to its source, stopping outside the dining room, which we'd already searched once and deemed empty. The tune ended as the call went to voicemail so Becca hung up to redial. After a pause, the drums and keyboard kicked in. Our eyes moved simultaneously to the same spot.

"Under the table?" Becca mouthed and I nodded, certain she was right.

A cloth hung so low over the side of the dining table that it almost brushed the carpet, completely shrouding the space beneath from view. We advanced together on tiptoes, Becca still clutching her cell, which continued to struggle heroically to make a connection with Tiff's. I ripped the cloth away in a move that sent the candlesticks perched on top clattering to the floor. There was a scream followed closely by a wail, and I dropped to my knees to see what the hell was going on down there. Instead of Tiff, I found the two Miranda girls cuddled together, the cell phone at their side.

"Ramona," I breathed, reaching towards the child so that I could draw her sister from her lap.

Although she was nearly six, Ramona was petite and I could tell that she struggled with the weight of the toddler sitting astride her legs. Sara reached out for me and I carefully drew her from their hiding place before standing to balance her on my hip. Becca extended a hand to help Ramona. She shook her head gravely. Her baby face was pinched, and her eyes were huge and wet. The very definition of terrified.

"Come on out, sweetie, you're okay," I coaxed, smoothing my hand over the back of Sara's head. She yawned with a squeak, using scrunched fists to swipe at her eyes. She should have been in her crib hours ago, not hiding underneath the dining table with her sister.

"I-is sh-sh-she out th-there?"

Ramona spoke with an uncharacteristic stutter and, from where I stood, I could see that she quivered like a plucked violin string.

"Tiff?"

She shook her head once more. I noted that she was already wearing her pyjamas and that she squeezed a stuffed panda bear tight between her knees. Tiff had made it at least part way through the bedtime routine, then.

"The lady. Is-is she g-gone?"

"What lady?"

It was Becca's turn to intervene, and she got down on hands and knees so that she was eye level with the frightened child. She forced a smile that I didn't think Ramona would fall for. She was a smart kid and Becca was pretty much a stranger to her. As I expected, Ramona stared at Becca's outstretched arm as though it was a scorpion. She shuffled back on her butt, skirting out of easy reach in case Becca decided to try to pull her out.

"What lady?" I repeated, struggling to drive exasperation from my tone. "And where's Tiff?"

Her thumb made its way to her mouth and Ramona sucked on it furiously for comfort; a move I hadn't seen her make for quite some time.

"The lady in the yard. She was scary." She spoke around the digit but, though her words were muffled, I could make them out fine.

Finally, Becca withdrew her hand and clambered to her feet. With a shrug and a look that suggested that I might have better luck, she reached for baby Sara. I passed the child off and she went willingly, far too exhausted to protest.

"I'll check if she has a pacifier in the kitchen," Becca offered, then she was gone, leaving me and Ramona alone to resolve the stalemate we'd somehow reached.

"Can you come out for me, sweetie?"

I plastered my brightest grin across my whole face, widening it until my cheeks ached. Ramona resolutely refused by scooting several more inches backwards. I decided to change tactics. For the time being Ramona was safe, and if she wanted to spend the rest of the week under the God-damn table then that was a problem for her parents. I only needed to know where Tiff had got to.

"Can you tell me about the lady?"

"Scary lady," she countered immediately, and her thumb fell from between her lips with a trail of drool clinging to it. "Saw her in the window."

"And what did Tiff do?"

My heart thundered. I tried my best to ignore it. There was probably a logical explanation for everything. I'd overreacted. I was on edge with Charlie and Mrs. Pedlow. It was to be expected.

"Tiffy went to look. Said she'd be right back."

Apparently, Tiff had spoken too soon.

"Did you see where she went? Did she go after the lady?"

Ramona seemed to hesitate. She grabbed her panda and dragged it to her chest, latching onto it so tight that her knuckles paled with the force. A tear squeezed itself from her eye and trickled down her cheek, igniting a roar of guilt inside me.

"Don't cry, honey. It'll be okay," I said, making promises I couldn't possibly keep.

"No. No." Ramona clung onto her stuffy as more tears spilled onto the front of her pyjama shirt. "I want Mommy."

I could identify. Suddenly, I wanted my mom, too. Unfortunately, I was the closest thing to an adult any of us had, and I didn't have the luxury of passing the buck to someone else.

"I can call Mommy." That was one promise I could follow through on. "First, I need you to tell me where Tiff is. Do you think you can do that for me? She might need my help."

I hoped she didn't. I hoped this was all some stupid, confusing series of mistakes that we could laugh about later.

With the promise of her mother's comforting arms dangled over her head like a proverbial carrot, Ramona seemed to arrive at a decision. Fingers working over Panda's fur, she stared straight into my eyes with the most haunted look I had ever seen.

"Scary lady was mad."

I waited, optimistic that patient silence would be enough to encourage Ramona to continue.

"She hurt Tiffy."

Alarm must have crossed my features because Ramona's whole body grew rigid. She glared at me, as though she expected me to react to her admission the way the 'scary lady' might have. When nothing happened, and I forced myself to remain motionless, Ramona relaxed.

"Then what happened?" I asked, softly.

I might have been afraid of the answer but I needed to hear it regardless.

"The lady took her away."

"Took her away?" I parroted, unable to help myself. Ramona glanced at me as if she'd already judged me an idiot, in that condescending way that only a small child is capable of.

"Through the fence."

"Over the fence," I corrected, reflexively. Ramona scowled.

"Through the fence," she reiterated more slowly, and I relented. I didn't have the energy to argue prepositions with a kid.

I remembered the fractured panel I'd stepped over to gain access to the yard. It had certainly looked like something had tried to go through it. *The wind*, I reminded myself. Just the wind.

"Mommy?" Ramona demanded, keen to ensure I held up my end of the bargain.

I searched through my contacts for Mrs. Miranda's number whilst Ramona and Panda held me under watchful gazes. All I could think about, however, was Tiffany; the last time I had seen her; the handful of berries she'd pulled out of her bag at the parlour; her ruined glasses that she would be near-blind without. As much as I didn't want to consider it, the more time that passed without my friend bursting through the door, the more likely it seemed that Ramona's initial assessment had been correct.

Tiff was gone.

8
DAY 4 – 16:32

We stayed home from school the next day to talk to the cops again. Tiff had never resurfaced; didn't call, didn't text, didn't come home. Her dads were frantic by the time they were summoned by Mr. and Mrs. Miranda, who were furious at having been called home from their date night because the babysitter had abandoned their children. Becca and I watched the four supposed-adults toss insults back and forth in the yard for almost twenty minutes before we managed to convince them to do something, aside from argue over who to blame. It was past one in the morning before we made it back home, where our parents waited with stricken expressions and fierce embraces. We were herded off to bed without discussion but Mom made it clear that we wouldn't be going to school.

In the morning, Becca and I both crawled out of our beds with our alarms – far too wired from the night before to sleep in. Mom offered to stay home from work, however, we waved away her concern, promising that we would be fine together. She also made us swear not to go out looking for Tiff, and we agreed. It wasn't like we had the first idea of where to start, anyway.

For most of the day, I caught up on homework whilst Becca

lay around the lounge, reading and watching TV. We didn't discuss Tiff or the Miranda house at all, not until the text came through from Rose after lunch.

"Meeting at Hayley's house again," Becca said as she checked her cell.

I set down my pen in favour of my phone. The group message from Rose scrolled across the screen. I swiped it away with one finger without reading. With Tiff gone, Hayley and Rose doubtlessly wanted to know the details.

I couldn't concentrate much after that so I shoved my homework back in my bag and joined Becca on the couch for a game of *Monopoly*. We had the London version, which we'd bought as a souvenir the one time we'd managed to make it to the capital with our parents. As usual, Becca swiped the double decker bus token and I pretended not to be salty about it. The clatter of the dice against the board each time we rolled started to work on my nerves, and it wasn't too long before I was chewing on the dry skin around my thumbnail. Becca scowled at me as soon as she noticed and swatted my hand before I could open a wound with my teeth.

"Would you quit that?"

I dropped my hand, guiltily, and tried to refocus my attention on the game. I was getting my ass kicked but that was nothing new. Becca had been the reigning *Monopoly* champ in our family for the past three years. It didn't appear as if my luck was going to change when I rolled a six that landed me straight in jail. We played until I went bankrupt, then Becca began to tidy the board away without performing her usual victory dance. I didn't question her low spirits because I wasn't doing much better myself. All I could think about was my missing friends; Charlie, Tiff, Charlie, Tiff – I was watching their faces whip past on a dizzying carousel ride.

"Do you think Tiffany went after Charlie?"

Surprised, I stared at my sister, who stood before me with the *Monopoly* box hugged to her chest.

"Why would she do that?" My lip curled at the absurdity. "She was in charge of kids. She's not stupid, Becca."

For a while, the Mirandas had thought she'd been exactly that. I was outraged then, too. Tiff was one of the most reliable people I'd met – the kind you could stake your life on. There was absolutely no way she would have left those girls alone and vulnerable. Not by choice. Regret bled into Becca's expression. She knew as well as I did that it was a dumb question but it was somehow so much easier to imagine Tiff was simply irresponsible as opposed to the alternative. We were both haunted by Ramona's explanation, and I could see that Becca was floundering to dismiss it. I shifted in my seat, turning my back on my sister, and she shuffled away to return the game to its spot.

An hour after school let out, we made our way over to Hayley's house. I kept my chin tucked into my chest as I walked, trying to avoid the stares from the neighbours who had already gotten wind of Tiff's disappearance. It was no secret that we were all friends: we roamed the Exchange, ordered milkshakes at the camp diner, and went bowling together. Always together, always laughing, until there was nothing left to laugh about. I couldn't help worrying over whether it was sympathy or suspicion that shone in their eyes when they regarded me.

Rose let us in. She shooed us upstairs to Hayley's room, where Mrs. Hill had been kind enough to set out a plate of hotdogs and a pitcher of lemonade. The buns were sloppily cut, like they'd been ripped in half with her bare hands instead of sliced, and the lemonade was sour enough that I suspected she'd forgotten to add the sugar, but it was progress. If Mrs. Hill was fixing snacks then she was no longer sobbing into her pillow all day. As a show of appreciation, I devoured two hotdogs and washed them down with half a glass of bitter soda.

"What happened last night? We know you were there."

Rose spoke whilst she picked apart a bread roll that she had no intention of eating. I realised with a prickle of irritation that my first assumption had been correct; they wanted all the gory details. Unfortunately, I wasn't in the mood for sharing.

"I'm sorry, we can't talk about it. Wouldn't want to spoil the investigation."

I leaned back against the wall, crossing my arms, and fixed Rose with a look that begged her to challenge me. Instead, she rolled a tiny piece of bread into a ball between her fingers then flicked it across the carpet. I was sure she wished she could get rid of me as easily.

"We're asking because we're worried," Hayley explained, and I almost caved when I glanced her way to note that her eyes were wet and red-rimmed.

Stubbornly, I remained silent. The hole in the edge of my left sock caught my eye and I worked diligently to shove my little toe through it so I had something else to focus on.

"Olly, don't be like that. You're not the only one who's lost people."

Becca didn't often scold me but, when she did, she made it count. Her words cut straight to my core, plunging in like a blade, until my breathing became shallow as a consequence of the awful pain. She was right, and I couldn't possibly deny it. Hayley, after all, had lost her sister, and there I was acting as if I had the monopoly on grief. It didn't help anymore to remind myself that my friends weren't proven to be dead when they weren't proven to be alive, either.

We delivered a recount of Tiff's last known minutes between us. I stopped to pull her glasses from my pocket and lay them out on the bed, where Hayley examined them.

"You're sure these are Tiff's?" Before I could nod or otherwise confirm, Rose leaned forward to poke at the frames gingerly with her pointer finger.

"You should have left these for the police. They're evidence, you know? Now your fingerprints are all over them."

"Evidence of what?" I barked, and Rose actually reeled back a few inches, like she hadn't been expecting my already frayed temper to snap.

"Whatever happened to Tiffany. You can't tell me that you - of all people - think she actually wandered off, right in the middle of babysitting, to meet up with Charlie, who – I might add - vanished off the face of the planet days ago?"

I didn't. Of course I didn't. But thinking about the other option was so much harder.

"When we got there, Ramona was talking about a scary lady. She said Tiff had seen her in the yard, too."

Becca drifted to my side and, despite our disagreement moments ago, I leaned into her. There was comfort in the familiar, and I chose to wrap it around me like a security blanket.

"Did you tell the police?"

I scowled at Rose, who seemed to make a habit of asking the most ridiculous questions.

"Of course we did. Not that it did any good."

"What does that mean?"

"They think Tiff ran away, like Charlie," I admitted, picking at my cuticles to avoid looking at the others. "There was no evidence that anyone had been in the yard, except for me and Becca."

"But she left all her stuff behind," added Becca, "purse, make up, wallet, phone. If I was going to run away then I'd at least take those with me."

"Not if you were trying to throw everyone off," Hayley said, thoughtfully, as she stroked the frame of Tiff's glasses. "But I doubt she'd leave these behind. It doesn't make any sense."

My thoughts drifted back to Tiff's dads, both equally distraught when I'd called them from the Miranda house. Tiff had been placed with them as a foster child when she was two, and they'd fallen so in love with her that they'd decided to adopt her soon after. She was their pride and joy – their reason for living – and I had never seen a family so close. They wore matching outfits every year for their annual Christmas card picture, co-ordinated their costumes at Halloween, and all that embarrassing kind of stuff. Tiff could talk to her parents about anything, and she often did, so there wasn't a single reason I could think of for her to leave. She wouldn't have hurt them like that.

"Who was the last one to see her?" Rose's brows furrowed, as if she had actually started to worry for Tiff's safety.

I raised my hand, remembering the ice cream parlour.

"Did she seem like there was anything bothering her?" Hayley held out the glasses to me and I took them back without looking at them, only to jam them in my pocket.

"No. She was totally normal."

I didn't add that it was me who had been the one asking odd questions about ghosts and uninvited visions.

"She ordered her usual then she left to sit for the Mirandas."

Suddenly, I remembered the berries – the ones that had spilled out of Tiff's bag over the counter. It had seemed like nothing at the time but, now - with Tiff's name added to an ever-growing missing person list – it was starting to seem like something.

"Except..." I paused when every pair of eyes in the room zeroed in on me, "there was something a little weird. At the parlour, she went to grab her wallet and her purse was full of berries. Yew berries. She had no idea how they'd gotten there."

My friends and my sister stared at me, unblinking and without emotion, for long enough that I started to worry that I'd inadvertently said something crazy. Hayley was the first to recover, jumping off her mattress and heading right for her bedroom door like she had realised she had somewhere else to be.

"We need to search Charlie's room again," she said, firmly. "First, my sister disappears and we find berries under her bed, then Tiff goes missing after emptying a pile of them out of her bag. That's a strange coincidence, don't you think?"

I shrugged. It was kind of peculiar, I had to admit, and that was why I'd mentioned it, but I wasn't certain that we could read anything sinister into the presence of some berries. Irrespective, Hayley was determined. She barrelled into the hall without checking to see if the rest of us followed. We did, although Rose hung to the back, not completely convinced about the need to investigate. I understood her reluctance. She and Charlie weren't close, and the notes Hayley had shown us last time were enough to freak anyone out - not to mention how uncomfortable the alcohol had made us all. I wasn't exactly looking forward to the idea of pawing through Charlie's things and I was her best friend. I could only imagine that it must have felt so much worse from where Rose stood.

The door was closed but Hayley didn't stop this time before throwing it open and striding into Charlie's space. I tried to follow, however, as soon as I crossed the threshold of the room, I was hit by the most overpowering stench imaginable. Ahead of me, Hayley doubled over to gag whilst, behind me, Becca coughed and retreated into the hall. I clamped both hands over my nose and mouth, sickened to the pit of my stomach. Braver than the rest of us, Rose pushed forward, her sleeve covering her face, to fling open the windows. The fresh air that poured inside was no match for the mystery odour, and I battled the urge to join my sister in the corridor.

"What the hell?" Hayley choked as she staggered over to me, her cheeks flushing green.

I shook my head, reluctant to move my hands away from my face. Instead, I spoke into my fingers and my voice came out so muffled that I doubted anyone would understand it.

"Smells like something died in here."

I was being dramatic, of course. Whilst I had never knowingly experienced the stench of death before, I could imagine that it was something close to this dreadful, pervading odour: sharp, sour, intense, noxious. A curious mixture of all the worst things I had smelled in my life – boiled cabbage, excrement, and vomit, to name a few.

"How have your parents not smelled that?"

Becca hugged the wall opposite the door and I realised that she had no intention of coming back into Charlie's room.

"They don't come in here. I don't think they can face it."

Slowly, I lowered my hands, doing my best to breathe through the nausea. The open window was helping but not solving the problem completely.

"It's got to be coming from somewhere," said Rose, and her features knitted in rare determination.

Before Hayley could answer, Rose got down on her hands and knees, and started to crawl around the room like a dog. Every few shuffles, she sniffed alternately at the carpet or the air in a bid to discover the source of our mutual disgust. Hayley and I exchanged glances, silently agreeing to leave Rose to it. We'd have more success without her in our hair, anyway.

"What should we look for?" I asked, bringing the conversation back to our reason for being there. Hayley appeared stumped for a second.

Hesitantly, she suggested, "We could check for her diary? Maybe she knew what the berries meant."

"Maybe she put them there herself," called out Becca from

the hall, and Hayley's eyes brightened as though she hadn't considered that idea.

"Let's find out why."

We moved in opposite directions – Hayley toward the nightstand and me over towards the closet. I opened the double doors and stepped inside, immediately stumbling over the rows of shoes that lined the floor. The smell had managed to invade the wardrobe, and every one of Charlie's dresses and jackets hanging from the rail had soaked the odour into its fabric. My stomach executed a rebellious flip. Gingerly, I pushed aside hangers and rifled through pockets as Hayley removed drawers from the nightstand to turn their contents onto the carpet. The search had lasted minutes when Rose's yelp interrupted. I poked my head out and Hayley glanced away from the address book she had been rifling through. Even Becca leaned into the bedroom from the hall, although she made sure to pinch her nose and limit herself to breathing through her mouth.

"It's coming from behind here," Rose explained, already beginning to work at wiggling the dresser out from its spot against the wall.

Hayley went right back to her task but Becca darted to Rose to offer her help. Deciding I'd had enough of the smelly, confined space, I wandered over to watch as they heaved the dresser into the middle of the floor. Its absence revealed a hole the size of a basketball in the wall.

"Hayley, look at this," ordered Rose, stepping aside to exhibit the damage.

I crept closer, an odd prickle across the back of my neck warning me against crouching down right beside the hole, like Becca had.

"That definitely hasn't always been there."

Confused, Hayley came to stand beside me, her nose wrinkling when the stench rolled over us in waves. I clutched my stomach, gritted my teeth, and somehow managed not to hurl.

"Do you think there's something in there?" I ventured. Rose nodded whilst Hayley chewed her lip.

"You should look," Becca suggested as her eyes fastened on Hayley's face.

"What? Why do I have to look?"

"Because it's your house," my sister reasoned.

"Technically, it's my dad's house, so I'm fine with getting him in here."

With a long suffering sigh, Rose fell to her knees in front of the wall.

"Bloody hell, I'll do it!"

Becca and Hayley stopped bickering, content to watch Rose boldly stick her nose – or her hand, as the case turned out to be - where none of the rest of us dared. Without taking a moment to prepare herself, Rose flicked on her cell torch and thrust it into the abyss. Next, she pressed her cheek against the wall to allow herself the perfect view of the inside of the cavity. The rest of us waited with baited breath and poorly contained impatience.

There was no warning before Rose unleashed her stricken shriek; no subtle widening of the eyes, or sharp intake of breath, or tell-tale flinch away from the offending discovery. She just screamed – so loud and petrified that both Hayley and Becca joined in without knowing why.

It was a wonder that the continued screeching of three teenage girls didn't summon Hayley's parents, but they must have gone out because nobody came running to our aid. After a handful of seconds that passed like years, Rose bolted for the door. Finally, Becca and Hayley were shocked into silence, and the three of us stood around, gaping at each other.

"What the hell?" Becca gasped, at the same time that Hayley came to life and leapt into pursuit of Rose.

"Rose, come back!"

I heard the front door slam downstairs. Regardless, Hayley ducked out, leaving me and Becca alone in the presence of the discovery that had chilled Rose to her core. Rose, who was as cynical as she was logical, and who didn't scare easy. With a pit in my stomach, I realised that I had to know what she had found.

I picked up Rose's discarded cell phone and hunkered next to the hole, clenching my jaw before I peeked inside. I was so quick that Becca didn't have time to stop me, though I began to wish that someone had the instant my eyes landed on the mess. My guts lurched.

"What is it? What do you see?" Becca hopped from one foot to the other behind me, anxiety making her antsy.

"Hand me that scarf." I held out my free hand and wiggled my fingers.

On the outside, I might have seemed calm and collected, however, that was mostly for Becca's benefit. On the inside, I was already several paces ahead of Rose.

One of Charlie's scarves was in my outstretched hand quicker than I thought possible. She had a collection of the things, which she would thread through her trouser loops, knot into headbands, or wind around her neck. She kept them all in the bottom drawer of the nightstand that Hayley had already ransacked, leaving a tangle of colourful silk strings next to the bed. Once wrapped around my hand, the scarf formed a makeshift glove. There was no way I was going to allow my bare skin to make contact with the thing causing the God-awful stink that had crept into the corners and crevices of Charlie's bedroom. Reaching inside the hole, this time blindly, I gritted my teeth.

Magic slid free of his resting place to land on the carpet with a thump that toppled the perfume bottles on top of the dresser.

He'd always been a big boy but death had bloated his corpse to twice his typical size, stretching his once-pure-white fur so thin in patches that his skin was visible beneath - grey and unnaturally shiny.

The scarf clung to the body, adhered by whatever sticky fluid leaked from his pores, and I shook it off my hand in horror. Becca reeled, chin wobbling. I leaned away from poor Magic as far as I could. His eyes were open, covered by milky film, but I wasn't about to try to close them, no matter how much I wanted to.

"Look at his neck," whispered Becca, and I reluctantly did, despite the fact that all I wanted to do was wash my hands under the hot water until my skin blistered.

"Shit."

His neck had been opened, brutally and messily, and the fur on his chest was stained russet with blood. The wound had long dried out, which was a small mercy at best given the state of the rest of his body. A solitary fly wriggled from between the flaps of skin to take flight, awarding us a glimpse of a clutch of maggots nestled deep in the throat. Clearly, this was how Magic had died, or - more specifically – how he had been murdered.

With the cat sprawled limp on the floor, the effects of rigor mortis having passed, the smell was far worse than it had been before. The hotdogs swirled threateningly around my stomach and I pressed a hand to my abdomen, willing it to calm, whilst Becca grabbed a pillowcase to drape over the corpse. There was no way we could let Hayley catch sight of the remains of her beloved pet. Not when she had already been through so much.

"Do you think…" Becca began, once the temporary shroud had been arranged, and we stood with our heads pushed out the window to greedily suck in clean air.

Although she trailed off, unwilling to finish the question, I knew what she had wanted to ask; did I think Charlie had killed

Magic, stuffed him in the wall like some ghoulish prize and then lied to her family for weeks about it?

I swallowed, looking away so that I didn't have to meet her gaze. The evidence was overwhelming whether I wanted to accept it or not. And I had to accept it because it was becoming clearer the more we learned that Charlie hadn't been herself. Somehow, we'd failed to notice. Now, we were reaping the consequences.

With nothing else to say, I pulled my head inside, closed the window, and locked it behind me. Then, I jerked my thumb towards the swollen, gooey lump beneath the pillowcase, trying my best not to recall how warm Magic had felt when he'd curled up to sleep in my lap, or how he'd let me carry him around the house in my arms like a baby. That was all in the past. Like my friendship with Charlie.

"Come on," I instructed, blinking back tears. "Let's go bury the cat."

9

DAY 6 – 09:07 HRS

We laid Magic to rest in the backyard of the Hill's home, next to a rose bush that sprouted enormous cream buds in the summer. The rest of the evening had been spent comforting Hayley, who sobbed over the loss of her cat until her nose was blocked and her eyes were bloodshot. Nobody breathed a word of accusation against Charlie, however, we were all thinking it.

On Friday, Becca and I went back to school. Mom wasn't so keen on the idea until Dad suggested that some normality would be good for us. We stuck together during lunch, since I had no friends left in my own grade and Hayley was taking a few personal days at home with her family. That left Rose, who was a pale imitation of her usual self. She stumbled through the halls, ignoring us when we called her name, as if she was trapped in some impenetrable daydream. Maybe 'nightmare' was closer to the truth. Finding Magic had really done a number on her.

The four of us gathered in the post office parking lot on Saturday morning, dressed in hats, scarves, and mittens to guard against the brutality of the October weather. Hayley had called us together and, though Becca and I had both wanted to skip the meeting, we didn't. Dad had warned us against Mum's Woods and we didn't usually defy him over the major stuff. He had his reasons to be worried, I conceded as I eyed the remnants of the crime scene tape tied to the railings. First Charlie, then Mrs. Pedlow, followed by Tiff: links in a chain that was growing longer at an alarming rate.

"Why are we here?" Rose pushed the toe of her boot into the ground, disturbing the top layer of soil. Her eyes stayed low, watching her own foot scratch sigils into the dirt.

"Do you remember those stories from Friedman's class? The ones about the cats in the walls?"

It sounded strange, and Becca wrinkled her nose in revulsion. Rose continued scuffing her boot, hardly reacting beyond a mild wince to the idea. I remembered, though, and I nodded at Hayley to encourage her.

"What happened to Magic…" she stumbled over the name painfully before she was able to continue, "got me thinking about it."

I turned to Rose and Becca, "Around the time of the witch trials, people in this area believed that they could ward off evil by sealing a cat into the wall of their home as it was being built."

"Most of the time the cat was still alive." I didn't miss the bitter note in Hayley's voice.

Poor Magic certainly hadn't been alive when he'd been crammed inside Charlie's wall. I'd yet to decide if his gruesome death was a better deal than succumbing to dehydration or suffocation. Mostly, I tried not to think about it at all.

"Why would your crazy sister do that?"

We all turned to Rose, who stared at Hayley, challenging her to disagree with the insult. The problem was, she no longer could, no matter how much she might have wanted to.

"Think about those notes we found. All she'd written on them was 'Aggie'. She drew the 'twisted tree' and then she killed my cat to seal him up in her wall, probably to keep the witch away. Charlie was obsessed with Agnes Tippett and these woods."

"It's a story," Rose sniffed. "Agnes Tippett died hundreds of years ago, and she wasn't really a witch – just a stupid girl who said the wrong thing at the wrong time."

"What about the rest of the legend? The yew berries? The seven souls?"

Whilst Rose's nostrils flared and her features darkened, Hayley wasn't to be deterred.

"*And if the witch should ever wake, the souls of seven she will take, to pay the sum of Scratch's fee, that he might set her spirit free.*"

The wind burst through the trees, and Becca sidled closer to my side. Our eyes were on Rose and Hayley, who were locked in their standoff with no sign that either was prepared to back down.

"It's a nursery rhyme! It's been around for generations but that doesn't make it true. If you really believe our friends are being bumped off by a dead, three-hundred-year-old fortune teller then you're as psychotic as your sister."

I expected the slap. Rose didn't. The moment Hayley's gloved palm connected with her cheek, she stumbled back – not from the force of the blow but from shock. They'd never really fought before, to the best of my knowledge. This thing with Charlie and Tiff was bringing out the worst in us all.

"What the hell?" Rose yelled, hand caressing her cheek. Hayley's mitten must have dulled the impact but Rose looked ready to riot, regardless.

I moved forward at once to put myself in the centre of the drama, mainly to keep Rose and Hayley from literally killing each other. If there really was a witch in need of seven souls, then my friends appeared keen to add each other to her collection before the end of the afternoon.

"That's enough," I warned, holding out both hands to keep the two girls at bay. "Beating the crap out of each other isn't going to help. Our friends are missing and you're behaving like kids."

Chagrined, Hayley averted her gaze. Rose continued to massage her cheek, exclusively for show. Neither one of them made a move to apologise.

"What exactly do you think we're going to find in there?"

Becca caught Hayley's eye momentarily before she hooked her thumb towards the mouth of Mum's Woods.

"I don't know. Some sign that Charlie was there, maybe. I haven't really thought about the 'what'. I just need to see for myself. I thought you guys would have my back."

Rose had the grace to look guilty for a second, however, she still ground out through gritted teeth, "The police combed every inch of this camp. If there was some sort of clue or evidence in there, they'd have already found it."

She dropped her hand and concentrated on shoving it back into her mitten whilst Hayley tried her hardest to avoid looking over at her. I could see the tears swimming in Hayley's eyes. She blinked them away before Rose had the chance to notice.

"We'll do it. Of course we'll go with you.

Becca stepped forward to slide her arm around Hayley's waist. I felt my heart flutter in my chest, dread starting to set in at the prospect of stepping into those woods when they'd already been the cause of so much distress. *Witches and curses aren't real,* I reminded myself, though there was a menacing children's song playing on loop in my head that begged to differ.

To our collective surprise, Rose followed us into the woods. I could tell by the way Hayley's eyes widened infinitesimally that she had expected her to storm off following the row. I was at least grateful for the extra presence as we trudged further and further into the tress.

Mum's Woods had stood for as long as written records had been kept in Mildenhall. Once, way before the RAF or USAF had staked a claim on the land, they had stretched for kilometres, much farther than the eye could see: a thick blanket of spindly firs, proud horse chestnuts, and the sacred yews, which burgeoned with their toxic fruits. Thanks to greed and progress, all that remained of the woods was a patch of land the size of a couple of football fields, with a manmade track meandering through its heart. It was a popular route for joggers and dog walkers alike, as well as a playground for the more intrepid camp kids. My friends and I had played hide and seek in those woods on summer days, and gathered conkers and pine cones when the season had turned. As we cut through the shrubs, those fond memories swept away on the wind that disturbed the branches. I snuggled into my jacket, drawing my shoulders up around my ears, and resolved not to stray from the path. We stuck to the trail until we found the centre of the woods and, consequently, the deformed yew tree that seemed to have become the object of Charlie's fixation. I kept my promise to myself - boots planted firm - even as Becca and Hayley drifted away together.

The 'twisted tree' was the stuff of local legend, alongside the name Agnes Tippett. The consensus among Mildenhall natives was that the tree presided over the spot where Aggie had died, with several of its branches driven through her elbows and knees, staking her to the ground. Supposedly, when the villagers had returned for the body, they'd found that the once-typical tree had been reshaped. It had altered beyond comprehension or explanation, its trunk twisted around and around like interwoven threads of twine, to taper upwards to the clouds. It looked - to anyone who didn't know better - like a hand that reached out for retribution.

It was claimed that they'd buried her corpse beneath the

roots. To the best of my knowledge, nobody had ever been curious or dumb enough to confirm that.

"Do you see anything?" I called.

Becca and Hayley circled the tree, noses to the ground. They looked like bloodhounds, tracking a scent. My sister shook her head and, at my side, Rose scoffed.

"I told them this was a waste of time." I hated to admit that I agreed with her.

Maybe Charlie had started to believe in the stories about the witch and her quest to free herself from the devil's snare, but I didn't. Sure, I'd experienced some questionable things over the past few days, however, that didn't mean I'd tossed logic and reason out the window completely. Tiff had told me herself that stress could do weird things to the brain. That was all it was.

"Maybe we could make some fliers this weekend, take them to Bury, and hand them out? If Charlie - or Tiff - took a bus or train, then somebody may have seen them," I suggested to Rose.

She didn't answer but she looked at me and gently smiled, accepting my olive branch. The disappearances hadn't made the news, beyond the local papers. Runaways were apparently a dime a dozen the closer you got to big cities and the police just didn't have the resources to deal with them all. Nobody really knew to look out for our missing friends, so getting their faces out there was at least something constructive we could be doing with our time.

"Probably a lot more useful than poking around in the dirt next to a creepy, old tree."

I couldn't help returning the smile as I glanced sideways at Becca and Hayley, finding them crouched beside the tree with their hands pressed to the bark, like they were trying to commune with it or something. I snickered and my amusement transferred to Rose, who muffled a giggle with her fist. She grabbed my elbow, needing the moral support after the drama with Hayley, and I found sharp sadness piercing my gut as I realised that we were slowly but surely imploding. If we continued like this - arguing and angry and lashing out at each other - then there would be nothing left of our group in no time at all. Once the first few dominoes have fallen, it's usually impossible to keep the rest upright.

To my relief, we didn't hang around by the tree or in the woods itself for long. Hayley seemed to tire quickly of her fruitless hunt for evidence, and the rest of us were so freaked out by the mentions of Agnes that we were keen to return to the parking lot.

Rose and Hayley went their separate ways without saying goodbye to each other, leaving me and Becca to mull over what had happened. We started for home, talking softly about anything other than our friends, who were bringing more storm clouds than sunshine to our lives lately. At least siblings were forever. Except, in Hayley's case, maybe they weren't.

We weren't far from our front door, barely on the edge of the park in the centre of the square, when I shot out an arm to stop Becca. Little Ramona Miranda hung off the ladder of the slide whilst her mom watched from the bench, cradling a sleeping Sara to her chest. Our eyes ticked sideways, locking briefly, and then the two of us changed course towards the gate.

"Hi Mrs. Miranda," Becca trilled. She was immediately perky and polite, just the way other people's parents like. Our own parents had learned to be suspicious of such behaviour. In their experience, it reeked of trouble, with the faintest whiff of duplicity.

Mrs. Miranda smiled at us both, though it was a guarded. She hesitated before sliding along the bench to make room for my sister, who plopped down next to the woman as if they were old friends.

"We wanted to see how you and the kids were doing after everything."

"That's super sweet of you, Becca," said Mrs. Miranda, her voice low so as not to disturb the baby. "We're doing okay. Ramona's not sleeping well but I guess that's to be expected. Sara's too young to know what's going on."

I stood in my sister's shadow, listening and biding my time. It would take a while for Becca to drag Mrs. Miranda so deep into conversation that she became turned around by it, but I knew she could. If there was one thing I had unfailing faith in, it was my sister's ability to run her mouth.

By the time they were discussing plans for the upcoming Halloween house decorating competition, Mrs. Miranda was so engrossed in the conversation that a pterodactyl could have snatched Ramona off the swings without her noticing. Taking my cue, I skirted around the bench, staying out of Mrs. Miranda's field of vision, so that I could approach Ramona. There was no way I could ask all the questions I wanted to with a mom in the mix: they were too protective, and too concerned that the slightest upset might scar their baby for life. Really, it would be their own messed up take on parenting that would do that. It wasn't that I thought the Mirandas were bad parents, but I was no longer sure if they were good people. They'd been so eager to dismiss Tiff's disappearance and to think the worst of her when they'd happily trusted her with their children for months. I was angry on her behalf. I'd actually kind of enjoyed watching the two Mr. Evans' chewing out the couple until the cops had arrived on the scene.

Ramona caught sight of me as I rounded the front of the slide and she gave me a wave accompanied by an adorably cheeky grin. She might have been experiencing nightmares but it was clear that in the light of day she felt safe enough. Free to be a child, protected from harm by the adults around her - as all kids should be.

"Olly!" she cheered, and I set my finger against my lips so that she'd keep a lid on the volume.

"Your mommy is talking," I warned, pointing over to the bench, where Becca had managed to manoeuvre Mrs. Miranda's back to the play equipment.

"Mommy's always talking," she puffed, and I chuckled as she rolled her eyes before collapsing back onto the platform at the top of the slide. She lay there, spread-eagle, then turned her head towards mine so that we were face to face.

"Do you think that we could talk?" I asked, coyly, and she frowned at me as if I'd asked her if she wanted a trip to the dentist or a second helping of broccoli.

"About Tiffy?"

I nodded, holding my breath for a moment as the fear that Ramona would refuse to cooperate washed over me. Her expression was thoughtful, finger in her mouth and eyes crinkled, but nothing about it made me hopeful.

I decided to sweeten the deal. "I'll push you on the swing. High as you want to go."

"Okay!"

The frown melted away and Ramona threw herself head first down the slide at the speed of light. Before I could register her presence by my side, she was shoving her hand into mine, and I was forcing myself not to think about why her fingers were so very sticky. As good as my word, I pushed her fast and high as I dared, though I had insisted that she sit in the preschool swing.

"I'm a big girl," she protested as I shoved the back of the seat, sending her into orbit. She leaned against the harness, giggling and kicking her feet with her pigtails streaming out behind her.

"Oh I know." I gave the seat another shove. "That's why I

wanted to talk to you. I bet you know all kinds of stuff the grown-ups don't."

I pushed again, waiting for her to take the bait. Sure enough, she craned her neck so that she could look at me as the swing began to slow down. To placate her, I gave it a nudge.

"They never believe me. They say *'Mona, don't fib'* and *'Mona, that's not right'*... but it is!"

I made a sympathetic sound behind my forced smile, my stomach starting to somersault.

"I believe you," I murmured. "I don't think you fib, or get it wrong."

"I don't," she said, so firmly that – if it hadn't been for the gnawing unease in my gut – I would have laughed for sure.

"Do they think you lied about Tiff?"

Glancing pointedly at the swing, which had glided to a halt, Ramona sealed her lips tight. Taking the not-so-subtle hint, I pulled on the ropes to draw the seat back then let it go with minimal force. Ramona squirmed in delight and I urged my impatience back down to lodge in my throat, where it might be contained.

"Yep," she said, though she didn't look back at me. "I tell Mommy, and I tell Daddy, but they said I was con-foosh-ed."

"Confused," I corrected, automatically. Ramona ignored me and my unwarranted assistance in favour of sticking her tongue out of her mouth to taste the breeze.

"What do they think you're confused about?" I prodded, once enough time had passed that I began to worry that Becca was losing her hold over Mrs. Miranda. Several times I'd noticed the woman poised to turn around, and Becca had barely managed to stop her – once resorting to grabbing her hand. Short of stealing the baby right out of her arms and running off, there wasn't much else she could do to hold the woman at bay.

"The lady."

"The scary one?" I checked. "What about her?"

"Mommy say she wasn't there. But she was! I sawed her."

From the bench, Becca was shooting me glances that ranged from desperate to pleading. Her message was loud and clear, but I hadn't got what I needed from Ramona yet. I refused to give in when I could be so close. Making a quick decision, I stopped the swing, silencing any pending objections when I dropped down to my knees in front of Ramona. She stared into my eyes and I noted that a surprising intelligence was reflected back at me. She reached out to pat my cheek with one small, tacky hand, and I leaned into the touch because it felt like I needed it.

"What did the lady look like, Ramona? I know it's hard to talk about this stuff, but I really need to know because... maybe I can help Tiff. You want that, right?"

Without hesitation, she bobbed her head – those enormous eyes filling with moisture and sorrow.

"Tiffy's nice. She reads to me and plays and gives me candy right before bed."

I smirked. It was so like Tiff to bribe the kids into going to sleep. She often said or did what the rest of us dared not to, and I missed that so much more than I had ever realised I would. God, I wanted my friend back.

"She is nice. And, right now, she needs us, so you have to tell me what you saw. I swear you won't get into trouble. I won't tell Mommy."

"You won't tell nobody?"

I would. Of course I'd tell Becca, Hayley, and Rose as soon as I was able. But Ramona didn't need to know that. No matter what it took, I had to get her to talk. Feeling like a piece of shit for manipulating a child, I linked my pinkie with hers and raised our interlocked hands in front of our faces. Pinkie promise: the unbreakable covenant of the playground.

"Tiffy was making popcorn. We were gonna watch a movie. Mommy said bedtime but Tiffy said we could!"

Willing Ramona to stumble through her story faster, I shot her an encouraging smile.

"There was a sound outside. I got scared. The light went off so Tiffy went to get a flashlight."

My stomach cramped as a tear rolled down Ramona's cheek, and my hand shot out to rest on her knee.

"The lady came to the window."

"What did she look like?" I repeated, wincing when I heard Mrs. Miranda sharply call Ramona's name. Time was up.

"Her skin was white," she said, poking at her own brown thigh experimentally before looking at me, "not white like *Elsa*. White like *Olaf*."

Another yell from by the bench, joined by the sound of Becca raising her voice jovially as she tried to coax Mrs. Miranda back into sitting. The woman wasn't having any of it, and I registered heels striking tarmac with dread.

"Her hair was like this," she wound her arms either side of her head, miming curls, then reached out to stroke my dark hair, " 'cept it was orange. And her arms and legs were hurt..."

"Hurt? How?" I grabbed onto the front of the swing seat like I expected Mrs. Miranda to try to physically haul me away.

"They were the wrong way. She walked on her hands and her feet, like a big old spider."

I felt like a thousand of the damn things scuttled across my spine as I shuddered. Ramona's face pinched with the kind of dread that comes with being forced to recall the worst moments of your life. I didn't allow the guilt in. If I did, I'd never know what had happened.

"What else?" I asked, at the same time that Mrs. Miranda called, *"Ramona Isabel Miranda, would you get your butt here right now?"*

Ramona began to wriggle in the seat, trying her best to get down, and I knew there was no way I could stop her without igniting Mrs. Miranda's ire like a bush fire. Instead, I latched onto the child's waist, pretending to help her from the swing to buy us a few precious seconds.

"She was mean. Her face was mad. She try to break the window. Tiffy went to tell her go 'way. I heard... I heard a scream. I hid with Sara."

I knew the rest. Tiff had never come back. Might never come back. Might be gone forever.

For a hint of a second, Ramona rested her cheek against my shoulder as I hefted her out of the seat and hugged her close to my body. I breathed in the intermingling scents of apple juice and *Play-Doh* that clung to her skin, drawing comfort for myself from the innocence of it all, before I set her down on the ground.

"I didn't like her," she told me, solemnly, "and I want Tiffy to come back."

"Me too, sweetie," I replied as I gulped in fresh air to ward off the tears that sprang to my eyes.

I watched her run back to her mother, satisfied that I'd received the truth but dismayed that she'd had to live through it. There wasn't anything I could do about that, so I pushed it aside. I had bigger issues to deal with. Specifically, the prospect that maybe Agnes Tippett *had* crawled right out of her grave, after all.

Becca listened to me relay Ramona's testimony as soon as we got home. She stayed quiet for a while, chewing over the information, before she offered her opinion.

"She's a kid, Olly. Maybe her parents are right and she is confused. Maybe she thinks she saw something because it was dark and she was afraid."

"She had no reason to be afraid; she was with Tiff. They

were going to watch a movie and eat popcorn." I defended, unable to help the frustration seeping into my voice.

After a moment of hesitation, Becca reached out to squeeze my shoulder, and then she subdued me with a look that I couldn't flinch away from.

"I think we both need to take some time away from all this. A lot of crazy stuff has happened around here the last week. We need to step back, take a deep breath, and not get caught up in theories and stories."

There wasn't much else I could say to that. Becca had made up her mind that she wouldn't consider that the legends could be real, and I was sure that there would be no changing it. She was as stubborn as me, and I'd already decided on what I thought. Unfortunately, this time, the two of us were at odds.

"Okay," I lied, smiling to sell it. "I promise I'll shut up about it."

"And you'll leave Charlie and Tiff to the cops?"

"Yep," I said. "They're the experts, right?"

Behind my back, my fingers were crossed, but Becca had no way of knowing that. She reached for a hug and I went willingly. I wasn't mad at my sister for thinking crazy things sounded crazy, but I was slightly disappointed that she wouldn't allow herself to see the bigger picture. Two missing persons and one suspicious death in a handful of days was more than a coincidence. Throw in a mutilated cat in the wall, the poisonous berries that were cropping up everywhere, and the pages of crazy ramblings we'd found in Charlie's room, and I was all but convinced that there were things going on at Mildenhall that I'd never considered possible. And, if the spirit of Agnes Tippett was behind them, I wasn't going to stop until I knew how to return her to her lonely grave.

If my sister wasn't prepared to help, I might have to do it alone.

10

DAY 6 – 18:30 HRS

Although we attended an English high school, the faculty were pretty good at rolling out the red carpet for us Americans, despite the fact that we accounted for less than half the student body at King Edward Academy. By decree of the principal, doughy-Doherty, we were actively encouraged to incorporate aspects of our culture into school life. As a result, we'd introduced our English friends to Sadie Hawkins, Juneteenth, and – more controversially – Independence Day. They mostly loved it, enjoying the excuse to add more celebrations to their calendar.

The cheerleading squad had been thrown into the mix over a decade before I'd arrived. They leant their support to the soccer and basketball teams, as well as competed in national gymnastics tournaments on the side - bringing home more trophies than any of the male dominated sports teams did. The Academy had really gone all in on it, with the construction of an outdoor bleacher system beside the soccer field plus additional funding for squad uniforms and a qualified coach.

Cheerleading had never been my thing - or Tiff's or Charlie's - but Becca, Hayley, and even Rose, were big on school spirit. Hayley served as the newly appointed vice-captain, having missed out on making captain by a hair. Becca and Rose were happy enough to blend into the background, so long as they got to execute the occasional handspring and shake their pompoms. It all seemed kind of ridiculous to me. Nonetheless, I tried not to judge since I was equally absorbed in my music. Outside of watching movies, Charlie didn't really have a hobby of her own, and I could only assume that was why she'd been so easily sucked into the whole internet-paranormal-chatroom garbage. Maybe if she'd spent less time online and more time forming letters with her body then she wouldn't have been missing.

The Warlocks were a decent soccer team so most of us showed up to watch their games when they played on home turf. The competing teams enjoyed the fact that – in the spirit of Uncle Sam – our teachers operated a concession stand. It wasn't anything ostentatious but it was more than most schools had, so we gladly stumped up the cash for limp fries and off-brand soda.

I'd thought that - considering two students were AWOL - Saturday night's game might have been cancelled. I was wrong. Mrs. Doherty stood at the gate, handing out missing person fliers, but otherwise it was business as usual. I should have felt bitter about it, however, I'd decided to give myself the night off from negativity. Instead, I settled onto the front row of the bleachers with my popcorn, and told myself that I'd become absorbed by the game (and Owen Stanley's ass) if it was the last thing I did. I missed having Tiff and Charlie at my side fiercely but I could force myself not to think about it for one night.

The floodlights bathed the pitch and the stands started to fill, whilst the cheerleaders and soccer players stretched their limbs out front. I ate my popcorn and tried not to look too pathetic on my own. Naturally, with nobody to talk to, my eyes wandered. I found Becca, Hayley, and Rose first, and watched them fuss over each other's uniforms for a spell. Then, I sought out Owen, who was hanging off a teammate's neck with one arm whilst trying to ruffle the boy's hair with his fist. As a person, I guess he needed some work, but that definitely didn't stop me appreciating his finer physical assets.

Cheerleaders and soccer players merged together; a mass of undulating, polyester clad bodies, all purple and white. Academy colours. The opposing team hadn't arrived so everyone else talked and laughed amongst themselves when the novelty of strutting in front of their audience wore off. Only one girl hung back. Not exactly atypical in high school, where not everyone can blend seamlessly into the right crowd. I *was* surprised to see that it was the squad captain, though. Jennifer-something. I'd never bothered learning her last name. We weren't friends and I didn't try out for the squad so it hadn't seemed necessary. I didn't hate her or anything even close, she just wasn't important to me.

That was about to change.

I watched her face, interest piqued by her reluctance to join her friends in the middle of the field. She appeared to be looking for someone, judging by the way her eyes scanned the crowd feverishly. I slipped a piece of popcorn past my lips and leaned forward to get a better view. Jennifer wrapped both arms around her abdomen, like she was trying to give herself a hug. Her front teeth sank into her bottom lip right as mine sank into an un-popped kernel, and I yelped when it splintered under the force. The shrapnel embedded itself in my mouth and I lost interest in Jennifer-whatever-her-name-was as I tried to fish it out with my fingernail and tongue. By the time I'd managed to wiggle the shell out of my gum, the other team had swarmed the field, and I forgot all about anything except the boy in the number twelve jersey. That remained true up until the half time whistle blew and the cheerleaders took centre stage whilst the soccer team filtered off-field to use the bathroom and discuss strategy.

The routine was one I'd watched my sister and Hayley practice a few times in the Hills' yard – Charlie and I lying back in the grass and clapping out the rhythm to the rock song. I was pretty good at that, given my musicality. To be fair, the squad wasn't terrible, either, and I found that knowing the exact order of their moves didn't affect my awe as I watched them pull off a run of straight-legged cartwheels, one after the other. Parents, teachers, and fellow students applauded for them much more enthusiastically than they had for the soccer team, who were losing 5-1. Grinning, caught up in the moment, I didn't notice when Jennifer's movements stopped hitting the beat. In fact, it wasn't until the rest of the girls dropped into the splits, leaving Jennifer standing in the centre of the pitch – a single frozen figure – that I realised anything was wrong.

I couldn't hear above the music so I glanced around to check whether anyone else was seeing what I was. Nobody appeared to have noticed Jennifer, in her place at the end of the line, standing stock-still, pompoms discarded at her heels. The rest of the squad jumped to their feet and Jennifer was shot a few dirty looks as she was corralled into her next spot. She went without resistance but the scared look on her face never wavered. The cords in her neck strained visibly.

She moved into the bottom right corner of a tight triangle with Becca and another girl, and I watched with niggling uncertainty as Hayley ran round back to put her hands on their shoulders. They were going to pull off a move that Becca called a 'basket toss', where a fourth cheerleader would be thrown into the air then caught in a sitting position. Hayley was probably one of the smallest girls on the squad so it made sense that she'd be the one airborne. Around them, three other groups adopted similar stances, preparing to execute the same move, as a few other squad members danced in the middle.

It was all fine, at first. Hayley used Jennifer and Becca's interlocked arms as a springboard to launch herself into the air, soaring to an impressive height. From there, it went downhill. As soon as Becca and Jennifer stepped back - my sister with her arms ready to receive her human cargo - the cheer-captain locked up like a corpse in the throes of rigor mortis. Her back stiffened; she stared straight ahead into the stands, fixating on something; then, she buried her fingers in her ponytail, and let loose a tortured scream.

Half of the crowd stood, collective gasps rising as we all realised what was about to happen. Jennifer fled the field, yanking strands of her hair out by the roots, but that wasn't the worst of it. Hayley was making a rapid descent to the ground without a second pair of arms to catch her.

I couldn't get out the cry brewing in my throat so I stood, silent and fretting, to watch Hayley hit the deck. The apex of the triangle had tried her best to take some of the weight of Hayley's body but she hadn't been nearly quick enough, and the three girls – my sister included – wound up as a tangle of limbs on the pitch. The impact couldn't be heard above the music, however, that cut out seconds later when someone pulled the plug.

I could taste my heart in my mouth – pulsing desperation and iron. I sprang from my seat and shoved my way along the row, reaching the centre of the bleacher steps as fast as I could. The crowd around me murmured, eyes glued to the field as the coaches and the principal ran to check on their students.

I knew Becca was okay as soon as I heard her curse as she crawled out from beneath Hayley, who lay sprawled on her back and gasping for breath, winded by the fall. The other cheerleader clutched at her left leg, weeping, and I thought I caught a glimpse of blood running down her calf. Maybe the glint of pale bone, too. I looked away before I could be certain. I'd seen enough gruesome things lately to last me a lifetime: I didn't need to add one more to the tally.

"It's broken. Call an ambulance," Coach Rhodes instructed a bystander as she wrapped her arm around the sobbing cheerleader. Cell phones appeared like she'd uttered magic words, then a fight ensued to be the first to dial the emergency services. The remaining cheerleaders closed ranks, shielding their sister from the eyes of the crowd. Nobody seemed to give a second thought to Jennifer, who had caused it all.

Hayley looked to have regained control of her breathing and was waving away the concern of the principal as she attempted to check on her injured friend. Guilt was written all over her face, and she hovered at the edge of the scene as she twisted the hem of her skirt around her thumb. I waited for my sister to stand and brush herself off, needing to be sure of her safety before I made a beeline for the stairs. Once she was steady on her feet again, I pounded down those steps and leaped off the last three. When my sneakers touched the ground, I veered straight for the indoor sports arena, sprinting at a speed that I hadn't realised I was capable of.

I was only minutes behind Jennifer and I figured that, despite being spooked, she'd grab her things before she left. She would almost certainly be heading for the girls' locker room. The door to the sports building swung inward with a dramatic creak, but that wasn't the only sound to cleave the gloom in two.

"Please! No, no, I haven't done anything wrong. Please!"

I followed Jennifer's disconcerting wails as if it wasn't the worst idea I'd ever had. The lights overhead were out but I didn't want to waste time hunting for the switches, and so I inched along the hall with only Jennifer's distress guiding me. I imagined it was like being blind, trying to cross the road, using nothing but the shrill tone of the signal box to help you, and knowing that you could be mowed down at any moment if it all went wrong. I was just waiting for the impact to take me out.

"You can't... no... no... no... nonononono!"

That did it; as Jennifer's moans intensified, the one word stretching and contorting until it far exceeded the single syllable it consisted of, I started to run again. Her voice was made of glass, so close to fracturing into a million pieces. It wavered, tremulous and tight, and I physically ached for her. She was beyond petrified.

I pushed my body as hard as I dared in the darkness, worried enough about stumbling over my laces or my feet that it slowed me. When I broke through the door into the changing room, the rush of the showers was the first thing that I noted. Beneath that, I could detect sobbing – the kind that doubles you over like a punch to the gut.

Newly determined, I navigated around lockers and benches, picking over gym bags and stray towels, in search of the showers. An archway with no door, through which steam billowed, seemed the likely option. My suspicions were confirmed when Jennifer's scream echoed from within. It drowned out the persistent pitter-patter of water hitting tile before it tailed off, as though it had never existed in the first place.

I tripped over a pair of sneakers, tossed carelessly to the floor, and almost took a spill. Righting myself with my hands on the wall, I managed to swing around the corner and into the showers, where I expected to find Jennifer huddled beneath one of the streams.

The room was empty.

Every shower was on full blast. So much water circled the drains that they were having trouble coping with the volume of it. It splashed off the floor onto my jeans, forcing me backwards.

She wasn't there.

All I could think of was Charlie's face in the beaker a few nights ago, and I shivered as my eyes were drawn to the puddles forming in the corners of the room. I turned away to continue the hunt, although everything had gone quiet, save for the hiss of hot water. No more screaming, no more hints as to where Jennifer had disappeared to.

"Jennifer?" My call went unanswered so I tried again, louder. "Jennifer? It's Olivia Sibley. Are you okay?"

Nothing.

I found her locker without much trouble: it had her name taped to it and the door hung half open as though someone had recently rifled through it. I gingerly pushed it all the way with one finger, thankful when I didn't find anything more sinister than a school bag lying on its side, a few cans of hairspray, and a box of tampons. I reached for the bag, which spewed books and pens, and tried to shove as much of the mess as I could back inside. However, I stopped when a handful of yew berries bounced against my fingers. Without thinking, I reached to gather them.

At eye level, scattered across my palm, they were innocent enough. Small, round, juicy-looking. Beneath that exterior, they were decidedly deadly. I swallowed, overtaken by foreboding of a magnitude that I had never experienced before. *Always with these berries.* The thought needled me, poking holes through which the last of my courage and level-headedness escaped. Could these really be the calling card of the witch, or was I buying into Charlie's bullshit?

"Jennifer, where the hell are you?"

The largest of the berries twitched, maybe disturbed by my breath or the trembling of my hand. Either way, it didn't register with me as anything out the ordinary. At the point I noticed that all fifteen of the berries were vibrating, rocking in my palm, and nudging each other, it was way too late. The first thin, hair-like protrusion slid from the centre of a single berry, followed by a second - a third - a fourth - all the way up until eight jointed appendages had emerged from within.

My stomach lunged. The rest of the berries followed suit

before my eyes; delicate, spindly legs sliding forth from the curve of their bellies so that they resembled a tiny army of spiders in my palm. No eyes, I noted, and no fangs – right before those *things* scuttled up my arm in unison.

Some went straight for my hair, tickling my face as they surged across my lips and nose. Others sought to disappear under the collar of my shirt, their legs furiously scrabbling at the cotton so they could slide their way inside. The worst of them made a dash for my ears, tempted by the promise of the warmth of my ear canals.

That was *my* cue to scream.

I howled like a banshee, wailing as the yew-spiders invaded the inches of my body. They were a plague, too impossibly fast to brush off, and too deft to prevent from reaching their destinations. They swarmed into my hair, vanishing into the curls, where I might never find them. A persistent one managed to wriggle into my shirt, followed closely by a companion, and I started to beat at my chest with my fists. I didn't care if I left bruises. Anything was better than this.

When the first creature reached my earlobe, latching on with its ugly legs, and beginning to push, push, push itself into the passage that would lead it within, my brain finally engaged. I threw my jacket from my shoulders and raced for the showers, toeing off my shoes as I went. I was far from steady in my panic, crashing into lockers and slamming my shins against the benches, but I was at least *fast*. I made it into the shower room and dove under the water without a thought for how hot it might have been.

I discovered that it was scalding. My shrieks of terror rapidly morphed into those of pain. Regardless, I rooted my feet to the spot, forcing my body into inaction as I tore the rest of my clothes off. When I was standing in my underwear, I shoved both hands into my hair and scratched until my scalp felt raw, desperate to dislodge the creatures that had taken residence there.

I hardly noticed how my brown skin had begun to pink, shining in patches as the water burned away the perfect layers. It didn't matter. Skin could recover but I had no way of knowing what those *things* could do to me.

I almost wept in relief when the plumpest of the pack plopped out of my hair and slapped the tile. Immediately, it was swept away on the current of water, straight to the drain. I scratched harder, grunting with effort, and more of the demonic berries dropped. Hope renewed by the sight of the things being sucked into the swirling abyss, I kept going. I counted them as they fell, some splatting on the floor in a pulpy mess, and others bouncing into the water to be carried away to the sewers. I prayed they'd drown – if they even breathed - though that wasn't my first concern. I had to rid my body of every last one of its invaders.

Fourteen.

In my frenzy, I managed to count fourteen, and my fear quadrupled as I realised that meant one was missing. A sharp scratching sensation drew my attention to my stomach and I screeched when I found the last of them burrowing inside my navel. Its front legs dug around, too deep, and a trickle of blood spilled out to stain my belly.

"No!"

I panicked at the sight, choking on the water that flooded my mouth. My hand shot out and I gripped the creature between my thumb and forefinger, crying out when I felt its wicked limbs sliding further into my flesh. It was trying to tunnel inside me - that much was clear – and I was certain that I'd rather drown myself in the shower water than find out what would happen once it succeeded.

"No, you don't," I ground out.

I squeezed my fingertips together, attempting to squash it. It was only a berry, after all, and I expected it to yield under the pressure. It didn't. It kept struggling, another leg joining the others in my bellybutton. With desperation coursing through me, urging my heart to keep pumping at an unprecedented rate, I barely noticed the gruff laughter ring out around me. It bounced off the four walls, attacking me from all sides, and I was sure that it was the witch - as sure as I was of my own name. She was mocking me, revelling in my distress, and waiting to see me fall. With a determined growl, low in my throat, I resolved that I would never give her that satisfaction.

I roared as I grabbed the crimson-arachnid-creature in my fist and pulled so hard that the several legs embedded in my skin snapped off its body. I might have imagined its agonised chitter, however, I didn't waste time wondering. The amputated legs fell from the wound, filling me with a relief that I didn't allow myself to enjoy. It died with a wet squelch and a very real moan when I slammed it into the wall, my palm covering it. Panting, I pulled my hand back to observe the result. The sticky residue of the nightmare clogged the lines in my skin, looking too much like blood to bring me any comfort. My shoulders sagged. The water petered out both above me and around me. There was no more insidious laughter, either. All that I could hear was my pulse in my ears and my ragged breathing.

I stood in the shower for a minute, maybe two, waiting for my legs to quit shaking. Once I could stand without needing to cling to the wall, I stumbled for the lockers. Without towelling myself off, I threw on my clothes. I struggled to tug my jeans on my wet legs but I didn't stop trying until they were over my hips. I couldn't zip them – my body too raw and swollen from the punishing heat of the showers – so I pulled the tails of my shirt over the waistband to hide it. I was tense the whole time, waiting for the water or Jennifer's screaming or the baying laughter to restart, and not entirely certain which of those might be worse.

I didn't search for Jennifer when I was dressed, I simply ran from the locker room, looking as much of a jumbled mess on the outside as I felt on the inside.

It didn't matter, I told myself. There was nothing that I or anyone else could possibly do to help Jennifer-whatever-her-name-was.

Not now that Agnes Tippett had her.

Printed in Great Britain
by Amazon

For our children, who have challenged and inspired us to be the best versions of ourselves.

ABOUT THE AUTHORS

Natasha Black is the pen name of long-time friends, Natasha and Suzie, who met in Mallorca back in 2007. A slew of emails between them inspired the idea to co-write this novel, and they've been working on it ever since … and laughing about it. And crying. And screaming. And more laughing. Oh, how they laughed. Quite a few shots of vodka may have been consumed too.

Professional model, and eternal dreamer, Natasha, believes anything is possible if you have the courage to try. Between writing for luxury publications and managing her sustainable clothing brand, she pursues every goal she sets her mind to, feeling the fear and doing it anyway. This free-spirited global nomad has already lived in four different countries, across three continents … She also eats her weight in chocolate, daily.

Suzie, the founder of a charity for disadvantaged youths in Mallorca, finds exhilaration in pushing her boundaries. From sailing the Atlantic and becoming a certified boxing coach to conquering Kilimanjaro's summit and kayaking in crocodile-infested rainforests. She's the living, breathing definition of 'challenge accepted'. She's also an expert at lounging in her PJ's and perfecting her skills in extreme social avoidance.

Love, Life & Vodka, is their debut novel.
Both the storyline and characterisation are fictional.

"Life without friends is like a garden without flowers."

-Jean-Paul Sartre

KATE BUCHANAN

There was a moment. Perhaps no more than a few seconds when time felt suspended, like walking across a bridge and pausing in the middle, in no-man's-land; neither asleep nor awake. For a split second, Kate would feel disorientated; not fully aware of who she was, where she was, or where she'd come from. For a fleeting second, she felt adrift in the universe, like a wandering soul searching for its place in the cosmos. In these precious seconds, the past and present blended and she danced along the fine line between memories of London and the serenity of her island haven in Mallorca, though years had passed since she'd left the bustling city. She wasn't ready for consciousness yet. She liked this moment, on that bridge, suspended in time, before another day began, a gentle interlude, a chance to breathe before the world demanded her attention once again.

She could hear David beside her, breathing rhythmically. It wasn't a snore. She was lucky that he didn't snore, more like a little gurgle and a whoosh as he exhaled. She nudged him anyway, and he grunted. "Was I snoring?"

"No, just breathing."

He opened one eye and glared at her. "You woke me up for

breathing? Really! Last night you were making such a racket. I dreamt I was in an avalanche. It even crossed my mind whether I could drown out your noises with a pillow without killing you." He turned around and immediately seemed to drift back to sleep. Kate found it fascinating that he could do this; be awake one minute and then back to a deep sleep the next.

She squeezed her eyes shut and grappled around the bed, hoping to find her earplugs. Regardless of how far she shoved them into her ears, they'd always transition during the night and normally into one of David's orifices, his belly button being a favourite. If she could just find the plugs without waking him again, she could stay in this blissful place a little longer. Her hand glided over the sheets and inadvertently stroked David's back. She froze, hoping that she could still squeeze a few moments in before his penis got the wrong idea and jumped to attention. Too late. An arm reached out to bring her in closer and Kate's bridge moment was gone. She was awake.

"Come here," he whispered, slowly wiggling his body closer to hers.

"Go back to sleep. We don't have to get up. The girls have a fiesta today. No school. You can lie in," she said hopefully.

David's hand glided down to her bottom, his soft fingers slowly stroking her. She edged away. In reality, she wanted to curl into him; he smelt so good. It was a smell she couldn't describe, yet it was intoxicating and she was unable to resist. It lured her in closer. If only they could just cuddle sometimes. Why was it that every day seemed to start with David wanting sex?

"I was just looking for my little earplugs. Go back to sleep," she repeated.

"How about a big plug instead?" David said cheekily as he

reached down to grab his now erect penis, which had clearly made its way across his own bridge, ahead of his consciousness.

"I can't," Kate murmured.

David groaned, his eyes still closed, and rolled over.

She felt bad. "I'm going to the gym today," she clarified, hoping that this would be a valid enough excuse.

"Okay, Rocky," he mumbled, reaching behind to grab hold of her hand and wrap it around his now curled-up body. This was good. There would be no guilt trip today.

"Rocky?"

"Yeah, Rocky, the boxer. No sex before a fight."

Relieved that he wasn't upset with her, Kate folded herself into him. She planted little kisses on his back as she spooned him and breathed in his smell. She lay there for a moment and the sensation that she was back on the bridge returned. Light was streaming through a gap in the curtains and she could tell, without even getting up to draw them, that it was going to be yet another glorious day.

Her head hurt. She had the sensation that she was drowning in a vat of self-loathing and then remembered the two bottles of wine they'd consumed the night before when their friends Nigel and Ben had dropped in. Wine, what else? Her mind scrambled to find the missing pieces, like a child looking for shells on the beach. There had been wine and a bar of Fruit and Nut, and … an image of her eating cold roast potatoes from the fridge, materialised. She groaned. Cold, congealed roast potatoes, which had seemed like a good idea after the Fruit and Nut and alcohol. That would explain the vat of self-loathing. It was a good decision for her to go to the gym. She had procrastinated for weeks, but today was the day.

It was obvious she would not drift off again. Slipping silently out of the bed, Kate grabbed her pyjamas that she'd dropped in a puddle on the floor next to the bed, and hastily put them on. Seeing the puddle made her smile. David always said it was like a bucket of water had melted the wicked witch from *The Wizard of Oz*, turning her into nothing but a pile of clothes. David continued to make his little noises as she tiptoed out of the room, hoping that the girls were also still asleep. If she could just grab a few quiet moments to herself, to sip her beloved cup of tea before the noise and chaos that was the Buchanan household began, that would be marvellous.

Making her way as quietly as she could across the hallway, Kate attempted to navigate around the creaky floorboards, stopping outside Emily's bedroom at the top of the stairs. Gently she pushed the door ajar and smiled when she saw her daughters snuggled up together in the one bed. Whilst they always started off in their own bedrooms, during the night, Tali, her youngest, would often make her way into Emily's bed. Kate felt her heart explode with love; they looked so peaceful in this cherished moment before the arguments and noise. Closing the door with the precision of a heart surgeon performing an intricate manoeuvre, Kate sighed with pleasure. It was time for tea. Then, and with no procrastination, she was going to get the girls ready, into the car and off to the gym crèche. She was going to do this.

Sipping her tea as she hovered over the kitchen sink, Kate glanced out the window at the orange groves beyond. She watched, bewitched, as the first rays of sunshine painted the land with their golden brush. She felt almost peaceful. The view of the mountains mesmerised her. She never tired of it. So deep in thought was she that she didn't hear David enter the kitchen. Wrapping his arms around her from behind, he planted a kiss on the top of her head. Kate melted into the comforting embrace of his arms; his six foot three frame cocooning her tiny five foot two. Whilst the image might have looked comical to onlookers, it didn't matter to them; their souls had found each other, so any height difference was inconsequential.

Kate almost purred. A cup of tea and David cuddling her. If only she could suspend the moment.

"Why did you get up?" Kate asked, "There's no school today. After last night, I presumed you'd be itching to get started on the plans for Nigel and Ben's Cave conversion. I'm going to take the girls with me to the gym."

"Yes, I'm really excited about it. I've never made plans for a cave before. I'm going to go up to theirs later today to take a proper look, but before that, I'm on a secret mission."

"What mission?" Kate was confused.

David just winked. "You'll see shortly. I'll be back in twenty minutes. Will you still be here?"

"Probably. The girls are still sleeping."

David was already heading out of the kitchen when …

"MAMÁ," Tali's blood-curdling scream startled Kate.

Kate and David looked at each other.

"It didn't sound life threatening, just go on your secret mission. I'll deal with it."

Kate went to the bottom of the stairs and yelled up, "Come down, both of you! I'm making pancakes for breakfast."

That should do the trick, pancakes were the household treat and not usually offered midweek but Kate wanted to diffuse whichever World War was about to begin.

"MUMMMMMYYYYYYYY!" An even louder shriek, if that were at all possible, came from Emily, her eldest, reverberating through the house.

Kate yelled up the stairs once again, "Both of you come down!"

Seconds later, she heard the thumping of her eldest daughter as she stomped down the stairs.

"Tali used my toothbrush for her painting. Again!" Emily was quick to point the finger at her younger sister, holding up her toothbrush, which was indeed covered with red paint.

"No, no *es* me, *es* Emily," said Tali in her usual half-Spanish, half-English vocabulary, opening her eyes wider in a display of pure innocence, as she entered the kitchen.

"Aren't you going to tell her off, Mum? This is the second toothbrush she's used as a paintbrush." Her nose scrunched up with irritation and the smattering of freckles made her appear younger than her ten years merged.

Kate needed to diffuse the situation immediately. "Come on, Emily, help me make the pancakes. Tali, don't use Emily's toothbrush again for painting please and Emily, we have loads of spare toothbrushes under the sink in my bathroom."

"Hardly the point," Emily mumbled under her breath.

The pancakes offered the desired distraction and once they'd been devoured, Kate sent the girls upstairs to get ready. She was now highly motivated to get to the gym, especially as she'd shoved the leftover pancakes into her mouth rather than into the dustbin. What was wrong with her!

David materialised in the kitchen with a huge grin. Kate looked at him suspiciously.

"Guess what?" He met her gaze, still grinning.

"I have absolutely no idea, David. What?"

"You won't believe what I've bought the kids. Come to the car and help me."

Following David, Kate's brain whirled as she worried about

what he might have bought. It was most uncharacteristic of him to buy the girls anything that was required or functional.

As David opened the door to the back seat of the old Volvo, Kate peered in and gasped, "You ... you ... you bought a rabbit?"

By which time, David had manoeuvred himself to the front of the car and was opening the passenger door with the most annoying grin still slapped on his face. "No, I bought two rabbits." He pulled out a second fluffy creature, as if out of a magician's hat.

Kate looked down at the two little rabbits, one black with sticky-up ears and one white with long floppy ears. She was at a total loss for words, but moments later, they came tumbling out in full force. "What on earth were you thinking? We are not pet people, David. NOT PET PEOPLE. We agreed, no pets, and these are definitely PETS."

David continued to grin but said nothing, so Kate carried on ranting, her voice now rising several more decibels. "Are you out of your friggin' mind? I don't want rabbits, dogs or even a goldfish. Who's going to look after them?"

"The girls will. I will. You won't have to do a thing. Can't wait to see their faces, they're going to be so happy, just you wait and see." David's eyes glistened with excitement; when he was happy, they became an even deeper shade of green. Kate could often assess his mood purely based on the colour of his eyes. This was useful given that David was in the habit of keeping his emotions internalised, unlike Kate, who had no problem vocalising them at all.

"Harrumph," Kate mumbled as she turned away, intending to flounce back into the house.

"Where are you going?" David called out to her.

"Going to the gym with the girls."

"Aren't you going to help me?" David stood there, with all the innocence of a little boy.

"Um, that would be a no. You said I didn't have to do anything."

Just then, David's phone rang. He scurried past her. "Darling, important call ... can you get them sorted into their hutches, and then I'll come up and we can show the girls. It's going to be brill."

With that, he disappeared down into his office in the basement, leaving Kate to return to the car, which not only contained the two rabbits but an awful lot of rabbit paraphernalia: two hutches, hay, and even some fake carrot toys. *Bloody marvellous.* Was it not enough to spoil her children rotten? She now had two spoiled bunnies as well.

"YOU HAVE GOT TO BE KIDDING. YOU SAID I DIDN'T HAVE TO GET INVOLVED, YOU SAID THAT ONLY TEN SECONDS AGO."

Like an echo from afar, came David's response. "Sorry darling, important call. Money to earn. Kids to put through school. Rabbits to feed. Thanks hun."

Not a hundred percent sure what to do with the rabbits, she put one hutch by the carport and stuck the other in the garage for when it got too hot. They'd have to be outside pets; there was no way she was having them in the house. Kate looked at the bunnies, the bunnies looked at her.

"You may be bunnies, but you're going to need the constitution of an ox to survive in this household."

JAMIE KING

"You can go now," Jamie mumbled under her breath as she found her mind slowly coming into focus. The dimly lit room, however, was still on spin cycle. It was safe to say she had consumed a large volume of alcohol.

"Where you want me go?" Tomás asked, perplexed, his thick Spanish accent laced with the remnants of the night before. At least, she thought it was Tomás. Jamie's eyes, much like her mind, were still a blur. Her only clue that she was in the land of the living was her rapidly beating heart, as if she'd spotted an unsavoury ex at a friend's party, and was dutifully forced to stay.

"Home. You can go home now." Jamie felt the soft mattress beckoning her back to slumberland, the cool sheets a welcome antidote to the stifling heat in the room; she wasn't ready to face the day yet, and Tomás, who annoyingly seemed to be woven around her body, was just adding to the furnace. She needed him to leave already.

"I am in my home. You go at my house." Tomás was now staring at her—that much she could tell—his eyes practically boring a cavernous hole into the side of her face. Jamie opened one eye and stole a furtive glance his way. He didn't look impressed. His demeanour contorted like a toddler who'd just eaten broccoli for the first time. Remarkably, it didn't seem to take anything away from his delicious good looks. He still exuded all of his boyish charm beneath his displeasure.

"*Oh chico, lo siento,* I must have been dreaming; of course I don't mean you." Jamie quickly came to realise that she was not in fact in her own bed, but in the crisp white sheets of her spinning instructor. *Bugger.* Now she'd have to make small talk before escaping, especially as she was planning on going to his class later; it would be terribly awkward if she did her usual exit move. Despite fantasising about getting Tomás into bed since attending his first class, she hadn't decided whether she wanted a repeat performance yet. As with most things in her life, Jamie King got bored easily. And whilst she had a voracious appetite for the opposite sex, variety was key.

Tomás was pouting. His sweet plump lips purposely stuck out to make a point, and although they looked more primed for a kiss, Jamie resisted. His sun-lightened hair, like rich milk chocolate with streaks of caramel, flopped over his deep hazel eyes. Damn, he was cute and the smell of his golden skin—a heady concoction of sweat, sunscreen and cheap cologne—annoyingly, still alluring. As Jamie motioned to move, Tomás pulled her back in, tightening his stronghold around her body with every athletic limb, the heat from his body radiating like an old laptop. Jamie wriggled herself free. After three Sex on the Beaches, she'd lost count. Or was it sex on the beach plus cocktails? Now that she thought about it, she did feel a little sandy. Either way, everything was fuzzy. She needed to leave, and despite the resistance from Tomás, she successfully peeled him off and inched out of the bed.

"Noooo *cariño* ... stay with me!" Tomás's arm reached out to grab her, but only caught the air.

Jamie ignored him. Sunlight was peeking from behind one side of the long curtain, casting a stream of light across the centre of the room. Rubbing her eyes, she scanned the floor for her clothes, which seemed to be dotted randomly, almost decorating the minimalist space. She spotted her G-string brazenly lying on top of one of the dumbbells beside the bed. *Fuck, girl, what have you done? You love his classes.* Jamie slipped into the lacy black underwear and picked up what remained of her dignity. Clutching the clothes to her chest, she wandered backwards out of the room. Someone had once told her she had a 'curvaceous' bottom, and a girl doesn't forget something like that.

"Turn around so I can see your ass. I love your ass." Tomás was now lying on his front, his chin propped up on his hands, naked bar the big white smile he was now sporting.

Jamie turned around quickly, wiggling her bottom in Tomás's general direction to keep him happy before resuming her exit.

"*¡Guau!* I want just to bite it!" Tomás snapped his teeth in the air, like a mock shark attack.

The apartment was small, one-bedroom from what she could gather, and relatively sparse in furniture. Whilst it would not win any prizes for interior décor, it was clean and tidy enough to appease Jamie's OCD. The bathroom, however, which she was seeking, was disproportionately large. It didn't have a bath, but one of those oversized shower areas with a huge slab of glass between the water and the rest of the room. Jamie quickly locked the door and stepped onto the cool grey tiles, turning on the shower. *Arrrrgggghhhh!* The huge chrome rain shower head gushed cold water before she could regulate the temperature, or step out of the way. At least she was officially awake now. She added some warmth and enjoyed the water pounding against her skin as she gently leaned against the smooth marble, slowly piecing together the antics of the night.

* * *

Smoothing down the creases of her red mini dress as she stepped out of Tomás's apartment block and into the blazing sunshine, the corners of Jamie's mouth tilted up. God, she loved this place. Summertime and the living was real easy … as were the men. Stopping traffic as she crossed the road, a master in strappy heels, Jamie was on the receiving end of a flurry of wolf whistles, as a sea of eyes followed her. Ignoring the surrounding admirers and the odd *"¡Guapa!"* Jamie opened the door of her silver convertible Beetle and slid inside. Shades on, sounds on, she drove the fifteen minutes it took to get home before she would head to the gym. Everywhere in Mallorca seemed to be fifteen minutes away, any further, and it really was too much of an effort. For a small island, it was curious how most residents kept to their corner. Driving into the parking bay in front of her home, Jamie glanced at the clock on her console. She had exactly forty minutes before class. She wasn't in the mood to go inside. If only she'd packed her gym gear in her 'never know' bag, she could have gone directly. Unconsciously picking at the rose-coloured polish on her nails, she sighed and opened the car door. She'd make this quick.

* * *

Entering the large spinning studio, Jamie made a beeline for the same bike as always; a specific spot she'd claimed to the left of Tomás, granting her the perfect view of both him and the inevitably steamy wall-to-wall mirror behind him. And no one challenged it. Suddenly,

Tomás burst into the room and bounced onto the stage at the front, fiddling with the music system. Within moments, *Harder, Better, Faster, Stronger* by Daft Punk came on, and as the sounds filled the large room, ricocheting off the sky-high ceilings, the class started to spin. Sliding onto his bike, Tomás looked over at Jamie and winked. She wasn't sure if anyone noticed, but she didn't care. She was ready for her workout, which was always the highlight of her day. Losing herself in the music, in the spinning, in him.

"*¡Más fuerte, mas fuerte!*" yelled Tomás as he encouraged the class to push themselves harder. This was, after all, an advanced spin class.

You had enough 'fuerte' last night, Jamie thought, giggling to herself as she fixated on Tomás's firm torso and strong, thankfully unshaven legs, unlike the baby smooth pins of most cyclists.

"*¡Arriba, abajo, arriba, abajo!*" Tomás instructed, as the class lifted off their seats in unison, then down again over and over on repeat, like a giant octopus on LSD. Jamie could feel her thighs burning. She'd already had a good workout the previous night. Any more, and they'd surely ignite.

Jamie continued spinning, flashing Tomás one of her huge megawatt smiles as their eyes locked momentarily. And just like that, she was re-energised. There was a lot to be said for endorphins, and cute instructors. Glancing up at the clock, Jamie's heart sank. *Crap, there's only ten minutes left. I won't look at the clock again. I won't.*

Before long, the music slowed to a gentle, calming track, signalling that the cooldown had begun. Before she knew it, everyone was taking their last deep breaths and clapping. Vowing to return as soon as possible, she climbed off the bike as sensually as possible, as if it were the most natural thing in the world. And for Jamie King, it really was.

"*Gracias,* Tomás." She beamed as she deliberately brushed past him as she went to leave the studio. His tanned fingers reached out and gently grazed the base of her spine, on show between her new orange crop top and black low-rise leggings, clinging tightly to every inch of her sweat-drenched body. She wasn't sure if it was Tomás, the endorphins, or the pounding music in sync with her heart, which made her feel more aroused. Sexual tension was always intensified post workout; and another reason she found herself in class with increasing frequency. It was also likely how she ended up in Tomás's apartment. Gazing back at Tomás, she couldn't help but notice his beautiful physique was further enhanced with sparkling crystals of sweat and decided a repeat performance was definitely on the cards.

Jamie wasn't ready to leave the gym, so she ventured into the main area. Wandering over to the expansive room crammed with every contraption designed to mould you into shape, Jamie scanned the area with the precision of an eagle stalking her prey and found it to be disappointingly empty. Jamie's 'hot guy radar' was so sharp she could scan any room in seconds, even this vast state-of-the-art gym that wrapped around the pool area below, mezzanine-style. It wasn't quite lunchtime, as none of the locals seemed to be around. But she spotted someone, a woman, power walking on the treadmill. At first, Jamie noticed her hair. Even tied back in what appeared to be a little girl's Barbie scrunchie, it was so long it practically reached her bottom. Exceedingly dark and poker straight. Unusually straight, in fact, unlike her own jaw-length mop of curls, which had to be straightened into submission every day. Five minutes into a workout and there was zero chance of Jamie staying frizz-free. Yet here was a woman in a hot, sweaty gym without a frizz in sight. On closer inspection, she noticed that the